FEAR NOT EVIL

A novel by

Arturo Muñoz Vásquez

copyright @ Arturo Muñoz Vásquez 2015

All rights reserved by Arturo Muñoz Vásquez

ISBN 978-1-63452-834-4

9 781634 528344

Vasquetzal Publishing:

AUTHOR'S NOTE

What follows is a work of fiction. While some characters may borrow bits and pieces from people I have known, none of them are based on a real person. For better or for worse, I have to take all the responsibility for creating them. The backdrop to this murder mystery is the traditional veneration of ancestors observed in November during the Mexican celebration of El Día de los Muertos and the Chinese's Ching Ming festival observed 15 days from the Spring Equinox in April with candelabra rituals, including food, are ceremonially offered on altars to nurture the deceased in their journey through the afterlife.

Dedication:

To my wife, Sonya Fe who helped me stop writing about killing evil people by providing time and space for me to finish writing *FEAR NOT EVIL*. She is a passionate force of nature, as an artist, who throws herself into her art with the relentless single-mindedness of Picasso and Georgia O'Keefe and at the same time, she is someone who can light up a party, and make everyone feel like the most important person in the room. I enjoyed sprinkling her personality (which is bigger than life) in the female characters in this novel.

To Homer
my big brother
con cariño
Carl M. Vargas
7/16/16

Acknowledgements

In the fifteenth century, the Tlamatini, the wise men from different ethnic groups who shared a common language, Nahuatl, gathered at the palace of Tecayehuatzin in Tlaticpac, near Lago de Texcoco, México to discuss the possibility of thinking and saying "true words" on earth and after much debate they came to terms on one conclusion: "*Now, of friends; listen to the dream of a word; every spring it makes us live, the golden corn cools us, the reddish corn is made into a collar, we know at least that the hearts of our friends are true!*" [Cantares Mexicanos]

I want to thank *my friends* for their support while writing FEAR NOT EVIL. Paraphrasing the words of the Tlamatini, "I know that at least the hearts of my friends are true". I am fortunate to have such great friends. I especially want to acknowledge Shireen Miles for her tireless support, Dante Cervantes for the design of the front book cover, Leonardo Ceballos for the design of the back book cover, Jim Greco for always being there to help me, Semiramis Muñoz for the review of the Spanish language, I want to also thank Will Lee, and Steve Yee for their friendship. Lastly, I want to express my sincere gratitude to my sons, Simeon and Nataniel for their continued encouragement, and special Gracias to my brother, Cesar who took interest in guiding this project to fruition.

Preface

The setting of this murder mystery, *FEAR NOT EVIL* is the San Francisco Bay Area and neighboring counties, where two boys, best friends, grow up in an impoverished and violent environment where souls can be damaged forever. In this makeshift and transitory neighborhood of migrant workers, a mother's love is an important stabilizing factor in the well being of their children. Their mothers must fight to protect their children and help them preserve their humanity and regard for life. They must develop the necessary strength of character to cope with the harsh realities of an abusive childhood; experiences that can twist individuals into angry and violent people, or ...forge their souls to be generous and loving people.

There are a limited number of books and movies, which capture the joy, the physical and psychological brutality, the loss and the day-to-day dramas in the lives of migrant families in California's heartland. *FEAR NOT EVIL* is such a book. Not since Steinbeck's *Grapes of Wrath* has an author written so compellingly about these proud families, largely dependent upon the treatment of the farmers and the labor contractors who exploit their labor, not to mention the "coyotes," who gamble with the safety of their families as they are smuggled across the border in trucks, trunks of cars, and boats. This story begins just outside of Gilroy, in the Conejeras, a cluster of shacks, indistinguishable from other migrant farm worker camps. The story becomes even more interesting when two childhood friends from hard-working families in the Conejeras are launched into the world as ambitious young law enforcement professionals, caught up in the effort to solve one of the worst crime waves to affect the San Francisco Bay area; a vigilante killer who is dispensing his own sense of justice, executing serial killers and thwarting the best efforts of law enforcement to catch him.

Contents

Prologue

The rain was relentless. I looked out the window and could not see a thing, only the rain striking the windowpane. I could see mostly darkness and the reflection of the lamp next to my desk. The drawer on the right of the desk contained my notes from my work as a homicide investigator for the Berkeley Police Departments. The details of some of the cases rattled around in my head for months. One in particular, involving a serial killer case is worth telling.

I have been struggling with reasons why a person becomes a serial killer. I wondered, *with the exception of those who have sustained injury to the frontal lobe of the brain, how do others become serial killers? Was it due to their genetic makeup, passed on from one generation to the next; or was it their environment, physical or emotional abuse, o r perhaps the worst cause of all, neglect?* We all experience rage and inappropriate sexual instincts, yet we have internal controls that keep our inner monsters in check. The serial killers who cannot control their strong urge to kill eventually get caught, but some are so calculating that they are never apprehended.

The FBI defines serial murder as:

A minimum of three to four victims, with a "cooling off" period in between;

The killer is usually a stranger to the victim;

The murders reflect the perpetrator's need to sadistically dominate the victim, who may have "symbolic" value for the killer.

According to the FBI's statistics, the average serial killer is a white male from a lower-to-middle-class background, usually in his twenties or thirties. But as a detective trying to leave no stone unturned, I can't let such research prevent me from looking at possible exceptions.

More than a decade ago, I was assigned as lead investigator in the *Rose Cases*, an extremely high priority case involving homicides that appear to be connected. This case has been completely thwarting law enforcement agencies in the Bay Area for more than two decades. *I keep hoping to be the detective who cracks this case, even though the trail seems to have gone completely cold.*

As I walk the streets of San Francisco, San José, Oakland, or Gilroy, I can't help but think that the serial killer I am chasing could be any normal-looking person walking alongside me.

Detective, Diego de Campos, Berkeley Police Department

Chapter 1

Conejeras

Rabbit Hutches

The change of seasons filled the air, migratory birds darkened the sky, bringing with them signs of upcoming winds and rains denoting the end of one season, soon to follow the coming of another with Mexican farm workers filling the highways, bringing signs that harvest season is about to start. Labor contractors and "coyotes," the heartless souls who prey on undocumented workers, navigate them through the circuitous route to farms and labor camps, and back to their local barrios. The caravans of road weary trucks and cars followed each other as if they were all connected, weaving up and down forested mountains and valleys to finally arrive at their low-rent housing destination at the south end of Gilroy. They arrived before nightfall, unloaded and arranged their belongings and by sunrise, the caravan had transformed itself into a Mexican pueblo: the farm workers, being expert packers and movers by trade, readied the community for fiestas, birthday parties, and Sunday prayer.

The never-sleepers were out and about before the light made shadows: straightening out boxes, carts, bikes, and work tools, putting everything in its place. The self-proclaimed cooks woke up next to the smell of coffee that had been prepared by the never-sleepers. The children slept, while the men and young boys ate, and scurried off to the work that would await them every morning for the next three months.

The agricultural community of Gilroy, known as the "garlic capital of the world," required large numbers of migratory farm workers to harvest the plentiful fruit and vegetables grown there. Throughout Santa Clara County, small low-rent housing complexes were built for these workers. This encampment, a light blue housing complex south of town on the way to Hollister, was one of those complexes. The Mexican farm workers who migrated there referred to them as "Las Conejeras" because the cabins looked more like rabbit hutches than houses. Almost

4

everyone who lived in the small one-bedroom conejeras was somehow related: if not by blood, then by their common experience of having to uproot the family and move four to six times a year.

Diego de Campo's family of eight lived in the back unit, which had a small patch of grass. All the other one-bedroom units had only gravel parking and were stuffed with families of five to twelve people. The two units by the driveway were over-capacity with single men. In the unit by the mini-mart/cantina lived Diego's best friend Carlitos, his mother, Rosa, and father, Juan Carlos, and the owners of Rosa's Cantina. Diego, Carlitos and their families were the only permanent tenants living in the Conejeras. During the day, the families would go in and out of each other's conejera as if they lived in all of them, and then at nighttime each familia would return to its own conejera.

The young men in the single units came and went like water in a sieve; one could find a young man among them named José, Miguel, or Guadalupe-Lupe, and occasionally, a Jesús or "Chuey." While everyone didn't't particularly like every Jesús that came and went, no one dared to demonstrate any disrespect, or talk bad about them, for the name of Jesús carried with it unconditional respect. As for the women, the name that everyone anticipated of any female was María: María Elena, María Joséfina, Marielena, or Marilinda. One could win a bet that you could call a girl or a woman María and she would respond. Most women had the name María somewhere in their full name. Rosa is another name that has many derivatives: Rosario, Rosalinda, and Rosemary, and in the conejeras, there were more Rosas than Marías.

Across the street from the Conejeras, in front of the graveled driveway, was a two-story house with enough violence coming from it that it earned the reputation of a

"War Zone". People would walk four extra blocks to avoid going near Juan Mercado's house. The violence mainly involved the residents of the house, but on occasion, it would involve one of the single men living in the closest conejera. Johnny Mercado Junior, who bestowed his father's physical abuse on everybody, he didn't't care if the men he fought were twice his size and much older. Once, when Johnny was beating on an old man, a single man from the Conejeras defended the old man, so Johnny beat on him too.

On the evening of the first day of work, as the workers entered the driveway of the conejeras, they tasted the fresh tamales in the air they breathed. They sniffed the air and smiled at each other. Carlitos Santos called for his best friend from outside the front door, "*¡Diego!*" The smell of hot tamales announced his arrival through the cracks in the door and open windows before he knocked on the door. As in the drug culture, the first dozen tamales were free: a tradition Rosa had started as a way of welcoming the farm workers back to the conejeras. The second, and all future orders were a whopping fifteen dollars a dozen. The orders surely came, keeping Carlos and his mother busy every weekend for the next three months.

As customary, Carlitos came to Diego's conejera first, and announced what he did every time as he reached inside one of the buckets, unwrapped the wet cloth, and pulled out a hot steaming tamal:" *Ok, Diego! Swallow one whole, cause we have a lot of tamales to sell.*" Diego immediately inhaled it, like a bird swallows a fish in one gulp. Diego's role was to collect the money and keep the "books" and Carlitos' was to carry two heavy buckets of tamales. Carlos, a strong and sturdy-looking boy for his age, did not let anyone touch the buckets of hot tamales. He became satisfied with being the carrier, the go-for-it guy, and a friend you could count on.

With just a few words, Diego's mother, Rosario Flores de Campos, respectfully referred to as Doña Ro, assigned each conejera one course for the cena: One conejera had beans and rice, another the chili verde, and of course, Rosa's tamales. The single men's conejeras brought the ready-made stuff, nothing that had to be cooked: like drinks, fruit and candy. Every migrant worker who caravanned with her labor boss husband, Robert Campos, known to his workers as "Don Robo," found their way into Doña Ro's conejera to be blessed by her. She would make the sign of the cross with her fingers of her right hand, touch their foreheads and make another sign of the cross, *"En el nombre del Padre, del Hijo, y del Espiritú Santo."* After the blessing, they went into the different conejeras to select their menu for their primera cena, or first supper of this *Cosecha*, harvest; after-which they scattered about the conjeras, and ate a full course meal of Mexican food. The farmworkers ate the same way they slept, virtually on top of each other. The weary travelers wobbled to find a place on the patch of grass where they could lay down and rest their full stomachs. The laughter slowly died down and manifested itself into an orchestra with heavy snoring and accompanied by cicharras, or locusts.

On the days that followed, Carlos and Diego hung out together. On weekends, when they had a lot of time, they played cops and robbers. Their first task was to find a hideout, a secret place that only the two of them knew about. Diego would say to Carlos, *"Our hideout is our secret, OK, Carlitos!"* Carlos would get mad for a little while because he didn't't like being called Carlitos, especially by his friends, but he didn't't mind adults calling him that. He was "Carlitos" to all his relatives. His mother had taught him to respect adults. He preferred to be called Carlos, but Diego still called him Carlitos with cariño, endearment and friendship.

Carlos practically lived at Diego's conejera. Doña Ro prepared a place for him at their dinner table. He slept over more nights than he slept at his own house. He was a light sleeper, the slightest noise would wake him, and he'd get up and take a look. Always on the lookout, that's Carlitos. Diego slept like a rock, except when his sisters invited their girl friends for a stay-over and due to the shortage of beds, some of them ended up sleeping on his bed. He preferred his older sister's friends; they kept their little secret and smiled at him warmly for having rubbed their naked legs as they gently fell asleep.

Resting deeply in a crowded nest, before having grown enough feathers to fly, a huge bird woke a baby bird and forced him out of the nest, It fell down from the sky, his wings were not developed enough to break the fall. Down, down, he fell.

"*Levántate, wake up, wake up!*" called Don Robo as he yanked Diego by the shoulder.

"*Stop me from falling, Don Robo,*" Diego begged before the vision of the fall vanished like a cumulus cloud that loses its whiteness.

"*Wake up, mijo, I need your help today,*" ordered Diego's father. Like all sixty of his workers, his children called Roberto de Campos "Don Robo," too. He stood Diego up so that he could dress himself. The girls were already up and they were at the table eating. After Diego dressed, a cup of café con leche, mostly leche, was put in one of his hands and a bag of lunch in the other. A group of men hopped onto the back of Robo's truck and the children fell asleep on the front seat. Diego slept all the way until the truck, followed by three others, turned onto a dirt road and finally parked near a blazing fire that was snapping with twisting orange and yellow flames; the workers faces appeared to be painted orange and yellow and with each passing minute a little more gray paint was added until the light of day and the fire pushed away the darkness; leaving behind silhouettes dancing slowly to a dying fire. Oddly, Robo's silhouette was much larger than all the others, yet most of the men were taller. Perhaps it was the hat that added size to his stature.

Don Robo, a labor contractor for the caravan of workers, sometimes contracted a job which needed twice the number of men to complete it within the agreed upon time. Robo had trained his workforce to be efficient by helping each other when needed: to work as one force and not as individuals. Miraculously, each time they managed to complete the work in less time than the contract had calculated. It was not only fearing what Robo might do if a contract was not finished in time, it was the fear of getting him mad at any level. When Robo was angry, he reminded them that he was the "Patrón." He would boost by telling his workers that he would take on a contract that needed three times the number of men because he had confidence in his workers. They worked like slaves and Robo often treated them as if they were his slaves. On and on again, under their wide brim hats, they worked this way because this is how proud men work. His motto was, we work hard because todos somos, *Hijos* de *la Chingada! We are all Sons of Bitches!*

On cold mornings, before picking cotton, to warm their hands, the men extended their hands toward the fire. The children squeezed in between the adults and they too, stretched their hand out towards the warmth of the fire and wiggled their fingers. The adults didn't like seeing the children work, but more and more the children were seen in the early mornings. Robo often was over heard saying, "¡Di *mi palabra!*" He repeated it in English to give the message more authority, "*I gave my word that we would finish by mid-June.*" Each contract had a set number of days. Wages were tied to the contract, but more importantly tied to how Robo treated them. Keeping Robo's "word" was having an adverse effect on the children: the more they worked to protect Robo's word, the more school they missed. But what else

9

could they do but work, they had to eat. The farmers were grateful that their crops were harvested by the agreed upon timelines. Robo exaggerated stories to control them and to skim money from the contracts. Robo pocketed two third of the money from contract. He displayed his disingenuous generosity on Friday and Saturday nights in the local cantinas. He often bought drinks and sometimes women for his workers. They drank and sang late into the night Some staggered back to their conejera as the light of day took away the definition of the shadows; others, like Robo, didn't return to their families until they had to show up for work the next day. And work was what defined them; the partying was their reward for their low self-esteem. In that celebration was a feeling and a sense that, here among friends, each of them were equal to each other, and as important as Don Robo or any other son of a bitch in the cantina. "Yeah! Ese hijo de la Chingada!"

Chapter 2

Berkeley, California

Berkeley, California; among the most globally influential small communities in the world, Berkeley emerges from the grassy shores of the San Francisco bay and ascends gently to the University of California campus and from there hurries up the hills where the wealthy and the chancellor of the university make their homes. It is a place where something is always happening to impact the collective consciousness of the time; it is a nucleus for thought and the home to George Smoot, winner of a 2006 Nobel Prize for physics. It is truly a place that can only exist in the minds of thinkers: Berkeley could have been named after any of the world's best-known philosophers: Kant, Plato, or Unamuno. This place is governed by ideas and their adherents: like those that led the national protest movement against Vietnam, and the ones that petitioned Congress to impeach George Walker Bush and Dick Cheney for going to war with Iraq.

Here in this place, with a view of San Francisco's Golden Gate Bridge, and with spectacular sunsets, God speaks to the minds that still have to eat and breathe. Here, the ideas come, they are in the air that men and women breathe and in the sunlight that warms their faces. It is often said, "You don't pick Berkeley, Berkeley chooses you." Students, teachers, and professors come here to discover that they were chosen to be here. Yes, even those that Cal Berkeley was not their first choice. That unspoken word, that somehow you were destined to hear at this point in time in your life: "Berkeley!"

*   *   *   *   *

The white gravel that covered the grounds made the light blue conejeras seem to glow in the moonlight. The trucks with canvas flatbeds and cars were all accounted for; no one was missing; friends and family were peacefully sleeping.

Diego de Campos, a homicide detective with the Berkeley Police Department, woke up in the middle of a childhood dream, leaving him in a warm state of bliss. For some inexplicable reason, living in the Conejeras was his most re-occurring dream. Although the de Campos family obtained year-around employment and moved to a house on 10th Street, it was the little house in the Conejeras that was his most memorable home. He knew that dreaming of Conejeras meant that he was going to have a good day. While he showered, he kept thinking of the people who had lived there. He kept in touch with his brothers and sisters; a picture of the entire family standing in front of a large oak tree with foliage as background rested proudly on his dresser. Diego wondered if those who had lived in the Conejeras dreamed fondly of those times as he did. As he combed his hair back so that he could set his hat on it, he thought of his best childhood friend, Carlos.

He recalled when his high school counselor, Mr. Anderson, a UC Berkeley alumnus, called Diego and Carlos to discuss their college choices. Mr. Anderson, knowing that the transient communities in the labor camps had children with untapped potential, he took it upon himself to advocate for them; assisting with admissions, scholarships and financial aide.

After brief salutations, Mr. Anderson said, "I have one full-ride scholarship from UC Berkeley for you Carlos Santos". Carlos smiled at Diego, hoping that they might end up together at Cal. The counselor leaned forward from his chair and continued looking directly at Carlos, "Berkeley is offering you a full-ride scholarship, son." He gave Carlos an envelope from UC Berkeley. "Congratulations, son!" he said as he extended his hand for a handshake. Carlos, in a state of bewilderment, shook his hand reluctantly and turned to look at his friend, thinking, "I hope Diego gets a scholarship, Diego deserves one too and we all know it." Carlos turned towards the empty corner of the room and wondered if his father had come, would he make an effort to stand next to him, and would he be proud of him? Carlos knew that his mother would be there for him throughout his life. He lowered his chin and despite his best efforts, his eyes filled with tears. Diego reached over and wrapped his arm around Carlos' shoulder and said in a mature tone, "Congratulations, Carlos Santos!"

"Wait! Don't start the celebration yet; there's more!" exclaimed Mr. Anderson, who had sat back down and picked up another three envelopes. Carlos and Diego stood on their toes. Their dream was about to come true, attend the same university for their college life. Good news had to follow Diego; he was ambitious and had the determination to be successful. The two boys were squirming with excitement about the opportunity to tell their friends and family that they were going to Berkeley! Their destiny seemed scripted, "Diego!" called Mr. Anderson, "you, Diego, have been offered wrestling scholarships by San Luis Obispo, Fresno State, and......... Berkeley." Diego was two-time state wrestling champ, and boosted with an overall academic profile that was stronger than most wrestlers. Berkeley wanted winners, not just champions. In the end, as it always happened, Berkeley chose Diego.

Diego remembered how happy he felt that both of them were going to Berkeley. They had worked hard for the scholarships: both were also active in clubs and other student activities. Diego was captain of his high school wrestling team, defensive captain of his football team and senior class president, Carlos had become his sidekick, helping out in school clubs while working before and after school.

14

Two years later, as good fortune would have it, Jimmy Mercado, the third member of his childhood little gang, the Hoppers join them at UC Berkeley on academic scholarship and doubled majored in criminology and biology. Jimmy joined Carlos at Diego's wrestling matches. The three friends thought that at Berkeley they would see each other more often. It didn't happen. Carlos attended some of the wrestling matches to witness Diego victoriously over come his opponents. The three met about a dozen times at the student union and occasionally Diego saw Carlos in the library, but that was it.

After their second year, Diego lost track of Carlos and Jimmy. When he inquired about them at Admissions, he learned that they were no longer registered students at Berkeley.

Whatever happened to them? It had already been more ten years since Diego and Carlos lived in the Conejeras. The times hanging out with Carlos and Jimmy were his best childhood memories.

Homicide detective Diego de Campos was enjoying a cup of coffee when his cellphone buzzed. The call interrupted his trip to memory lane. Diego was urgently dispatched to inspect a crime scene of a double homicide and possible rape at the Claremont Hotel.

"Double 187, possible 261, over."

Chapter 3

Fox Hole

Most boys grow up different than girls. Boys need friendships with other boys that are based on a common need to belong to a secret club: a secret society that creates its own history, develops its own code of ethics, and designs its own mythology with dragons to slay, battles to fight, and hideouts to disappear into. When Carlos and Diego were not busy selling tamales, the two boys were busy looking for a secret hideout where they could play cops and robber games. They ruled out a tree house, even though there were good trees in the neighborhood for one. To have a hideout up in a tree was too dangerous anyway; one of them could fall off and get seriously hurt. A hideout underneath the foundation of one of the conejeras was out of the question; it was too dirty and the smell of a decaying cat or rat kept the kids from crawling under it.

After a two-day rain, the tall grass in the empty lot between Johnny's house and the nearby ice cream warehouse was still too wet to be it. In an attempt to find a shortcut through the tall grass, the two boys trampled on the grass, and they quickly realized that the grass was taller than Carlitos, who was three inches taller than Diego. The idea of having a hideout in the tall grass came to both of them at about the same time. Diego looked at Carlitos and read his mind: the tall grass was hiding the two of them from the rest of the world.

Diego and Carlitos were excited that they had found a hideout. With their feet, they smashed down the grass, making a circle five feet in diameter, big enough to sit down in. Unfortunately, the wet grass instantly soaked through their pants. In their excitement, they dug a one-foot deep hole in the wet dirt with their hands. Before they realized what they had done, the idea of digging a hole in the ground for their hideout came to them again at the same time and they kept digging until their foxhole was large enough for both of them to sit down to play games and solve crimes. They used an abandoned door to cover up the foxhole. Next, the discussion revolved around whether they should call their club "Los Conejos" (Rabbits), "the Gophers," "the Moles," or "Los Zorros" (Foxes), but each name

18

was rejected by one of them. One late afternoon, before it started getting dark, they took flashlights to stay late. They were too busy talking to notice the crickets signaling fellow creatures that it was safe to join them. The soft wind died down, giving a false impression that the crickets were getting louder, when suddenly, a swarm of grasshoppers filled the night air, landing all around them, except in their foxhole. *"That's it! The name of our club shall be, "The Grasshoppers,"* exclaimed Carlitos.

Diego didn't object to the club name, "Humm," he thought out-loud, "yeah, the Hoppers!"

The Hoppers worked independently on supplying the foxhole with equipment to make weapons: swords to slay dragons and villains, wooden pistols and rifles to hunt imaginary prey, and lances to protect the foxhole. Carlitos carved a perfect V-shaped slingshot out of a tree branch. He later would become a slingshot sharpshooter, on target with every pebble. Carlitos envisioned himself as David and picked up the slingshot to slay Goliath or any other monster that they may encounter. He saw himself as an underdog that will always triumph over adversity; and it was this vision of himself that he used to focus on becoming a crime fighter.

For now, the Hoppers started planning their new mission: fighting crime and protecting the neighborhood. They adopted a prayer they learned in Catholic school, "In the presence of our enemies, we will *fear not evil*. For our Lord protects us because we are pure at heart." The foxhole was getting cluttered with weapons and the tin buckets used as chairs and tables, so the boys decided to expand the hideout. With a bucket, Carlitos dug a four-foot long tunnel below the surface of the ground. The tunnel was needed to store weapons and equipment. Within two months, they dug four more tunnels, so there was one for each of the cardinal directions.

Regrettably, the foxhole hideout was short-lived. In the summer months that followed, the grass and weeds became a fire hazard. The ice cream company owned the property and they hired someone to mow the grass. Halfway through the mowing, the worker drove mower into the foxhole. The hideout was badly damaged: the mower broke the door in two, and half-filled in the tunnels with dirt. By the time the police came to investigate, the warehouse crew had pulled the mower out with a backhoe and filled the tunnels and foxhole with dirt and grass. The police asked questions, but left when they noted that the mower had been pulled out of the hole in the empty lot and the hole and tunnels were filled with dirt.

Diego and Carlitos did not waste any time mourning the death of the foxhole because they now had a club name, the Grasshoppers. The Hoppers (the code name for the club) had to hop to another hideout. The boys' mission had turned into finding another hideout. Carlitos had a private hideout that only his mother knew about, but he would wait another ten months before he would share his secret with Diego. They filled the days that followed with planning and writing up case files: some that had bank robbers, others--Robin Hood-type characters--stealing from the rich and giving to the poor. The boys agreed they needed a safe place, but not an underground one, ever again. Diego didn't want to even imagine the outcome if the two of them had been in the foxhole when the mower drove over it. Diego and Carlitos wanted to find a place where they could stay up late at night, tell spy stories and plan crimes that only the Hoppers could solve. Diego usually came up with the story line and Carlos filled in the details. The two desperately needed a real crime to solve in order for them to feel that they were real cops, and that they were conducting real surveillance and police work.

Carlitos learned from his mother, Rosa that the neighborhood was complaining about a foul order coming from the back of the two-story house across the street from the Conejeras. When Diego heard about a potential case to solve, he and Carlitos immediately walked past the alley by the Mercados' two-story house. The Mercados' had two teenage boys, Johnny and Jimmy, about the same age as Diego and Carlitos and a younger sister, Coca.

20

That night, the two boys hopped onto the Mercados' back fence, and from there, climbed the tree in the backyard. Sure enough, the evidence was high enough to disguise it from the ground, but from their vantage point, the boys could see that a cat had been gutted from the throat to its rectum, stretched open and tied to the tree branches. Carlitos cut the cat down, and they buried it near the ole foxhole. The next day, early in the afternoon, the Hoppers were on duty, so they hopped onto the roof of the nearest conejera facing the two-story house. From the roof, they surveyed the area for more evidence of foul play. Just then, Juan Mercado came home and all hell broke loose, he started beating his kids for no any reason: being in his way, for eating food before he gave his approval to eat.. He picked on eleven-year old Jimmy the most, because he had lighter coloring than his brother and sister and he was the only one with Asian-looking features, "Chinito eyes," he taunted. Jimmy's face was always bruised. After staking out Mercado's house for three days, Diego and Carlitos deduced that Jimmy had killed the cat in retaliation for his father's verbal and physical abuse. They waited for Jimmy to be alone before they approached him. Saturday, when the neighborhood families went shopping for their weekly groceries, Jimmy stayed behind.

Carlitos and Diego called him to the alley, *"Hey! Jimmy!"* Jimmy came out to talk to them. He half-smiled, looking more than a little worried about the intent of the boys. The three boys walked down the alley a block before Diego spoke, *"We know you killed the cat!"*

Jimmy denied it. But just as quickly, his wounded heart caved in, and he started sobbing, almost choking. Jimmy bared his soul, "I didn't kill the cat, but I wanted to. My dad called the cat Junior; he loved the cat more than any of us. The cat was run over by Mr. Johnson, our next-door neighbor ran over the cat as he was backing up out of driveway. He never saw Junior. I was scared because I knew my dad would blame me. I kept Junior alive for several hours, but he died on me. I opened him up to see which organ failed him. Sooner or later, I know my father will

21

figure it out that "Junior" hasn't just wandered off and that won't be good. I wish my father had been run over instead."

"Diego, can Jimmy join our club?" pleaded Carlitos feeling 's empathy for Jimmy.

"Sure! You'll need a code name," Diego answered quickly. *"Your code name shall be Chino,"* Carlitos said, knowing that people already called him "Chino." "You can call me Smiley and Carlitos you can call me Carlos, el Tamalero. Everybody had names in the conejeras: Chivo" (Old Goat), "Cabeza de Vaca," "Garrapata (tick)," and"Chaparo (Shorty)."

The Grasshoppers created plenty of mystery to fill their minds with theories and solutions. And now with a third member, the boys decided they also needed a secret handshake, a hand signal, or wave. None of them remembered who started the Hoppers' grooming routine first; Carlos stroked his long imaginary whiskers, and Jimmy rubbed his feet together and Diego cleaned his wings. The three protectors of the barrio clasped their hands and repeated their motto: "Fear No Evil."

The manager at the warehouse behind Jimmy's house hired him to clean the bathrooms and empty the trashcans in exchange for a week's supply of ice cream for his family. Jimmy's family was known for being industrious. The boys and Coca, the youngest girl were skilled auto mechanics. After working at the ice cream warehouse in less than a week, Jimmy started unscrewing the nuts off the bolts to a corner panel of the metal building. One night, the Grasshoppers returned to the barbed wire fence that bordered the ice cream warehouse. Carlos and Diego were prepared to hop over the fence, but Jimmy had already cut enough wire to lift the fence a little and the Hoppers took small hops as they went under the fence. The Hoppers flew low all the way to the corner of the building. Jimmy pulled out four bolts suspending the panel and then wiggled it until it slid to one side, creating an opening large enough for them to squeeze through.

Jimmy had learned that no one went up the steps to the loft in the ice cream warehouse. Learning about the abandoned loft gave Jimmy the idea to suggest it as a possible hideout for the Hoppers. It was a perfect place to stay up late at night. The trio moved some boxes, metal barrels, and equipment to create their new hideout. With its boarded-up windows, the hideout was not visible to anyone. On the next visit, they came prepared with flashlights and a drawing of the head of a grasshopper designed by Jimmy. Two boys in battle gear are riding a giant green grasshopper and one with a flashlight is pulling them forward by the grasshopper's antenna. They pinned their Grasshopper's logo onto a cardboard box and started grooming themselves. They borrowed a lamp from one of the offices, and aimed the light at the head of the Grand Grasshopper and thereby officially initiated the Ice Cream hideout. The boys made up stories, some corny ones, but mostly criminal stories, which in their minds were the greatest murder mysteries of all time. Nobody ever caught on that when they mentioned, *Ice Cream*, they were referring to their new hideout. Their new greeting had evolved into simply holding their arms and shivering briefly. Jimmy bowed a little forward as he held his arms and shivered. Diego shivered with his eyes closed. They spent a lot of nights telling stories in the ice cream warehouse. To go back home or to end a stay anywhere, each of the three had to shiver in his particular way.

The three Hoppers had been in their Ice Cream hideout six months when one afternoon, on the way home from school, they noticed a yellow KEEP OUT sign on the fence. The gate entrance had a sign too, CLOSED in big letters. The Ice Cream company workers soon showed up with big flatbed trucks, dismantled the metal building and hauled it away to a new storage facility located by San Martín. After the city workers had left for the day, uninvited scavengers carried off everything else of any possible value: fencing, metal poles, and metal sidings.

It was all gone within twenty-four hours. To Carlos, Diego and Jimmy, it seemed like their childhood was stolen right in front of them and there was nothing they could do but accept that the hideout was now history.

The Hoppers stood there grooming as they looked at two empty lots: the ice cream warehouse and the foxhole lot. Carlos seemed older now, and the tall tales the three shared were no longer whirling in their minds. However, they still vowed to protect their community, the Conejeras against all evil, because they were pure at heart and they "Fear not Evil". Having a hideout seemed less important now. Their quest had become finding evil, no matter in who evil hid.

"Diego, I have a secret hideout to share with you, but you must promise one thing," said Carlos.

"Yeah! Anything," Diego replied.

"You can't make a sound, be real quiet, and you have to stay till morning," demanded Carlos.

"No problem, you are my best friend." Diego assured Carlos that he would keep it secret.

"One more thing, you can't tell Doña Ro, your mother." Diego nodded in agreement.

Chapter 4

Claremont Hotel

The Claremont Hotel Club is nestled up against the Oakland Hills in Berkeley. From many locations on its legendary twenty-two acre property, one can witness the red-orange towers of the Golden Gate bridge emerge out of the fog and hold up the rest of the sky, and in the evenings the spectacular views of the San Francisco Bay shimmer in orange-yellow lights against a dark night. During the late summer afternoons, the hotel looks more like a white palace with a gable tower chiseled out of white marble. Looking up at the massive dimensions of the hotel, one wonders how those silent partners who developed the property ever managed to accrue enough money to purchase such a lavish quantity of property. Imagine 279-guest accommodations that are plush, comfortable, luxurious, and modern.

The Claremont is a place where the idle rich hang out. Here, like in all international hotspots, the successful are pampered with winning cuisines, fitness complexes, hiking, tennis courts, and health therapy. The wealthy and the wanna-be wealthy come here to luxuriate in the comfortable surroundings, indulge their appetites, enrich their way of life, and to rub shoulders with people like themselves. The Claremont Hotel Club is where people come to experience the grace and elegance of perfection, a place where the air that fills one's lungs also fills the mind with fresh ideas. No question, those that come here fall in love with the quality of life that the Claremont Hotel Club offers its members and guests.

*   *   *   *

At the entrance to the hotel, the gates were upright and opened; two police cars with their flashing red and blue lights guarded against anyone from going in and out without permission from Captain Williams. The entire Claremont was on lockdown by the Berkeley police. The officers and their K-9 partners were dispatched to check the hotel's entire property. The sun cast its light on the white walls of the hotel giving the appearance of a monastery rather than a hotel. The Claremont Hotel gave the appearance that it was casting its own light. Behind the hotel, four tennis courts were in use. The players, much accustomed to dictating the terms of any arrangement, insisted on completing their sets before being interrogated by the police. The grunts by the tennis players hitting the ball back and forth echoed up the hill to the back entrance of the hotel.

"Ugh!"

"Aah!"

"Ugh!"

"Aah!"

"Ugh!"

"Aah!"

"Ugh!"

Inside the hotel, the police separated the employees and escorted them to separate ballrooms. Some of the guests were directed to stay in their rooms until further notice.

Diego de Campos, a homicide detective for the police department drove up to the gate, and the security detail waved him through. Diego noted the number of police on the grounds of the hotel. Once inside, he was escorted to the elevator, where he went to the third floor. The elevator announced the opening of the door with a loud "ding." Inside the suite where the homicide had taken place, forensics staff was busy collecting evidence.

A detective standing next to the yellow tape informed Diego, *"a double 187, a white female in the bathroom and a white male in the bedroom. The woman floating in the bathtub with soapy water and blood appeared to be about five feet four, weighed one hundred and thirty pounds and she was about fifty years old."*

Diego inspected the multiple knife wounds on her chest, and the forensics officer's badge, and then replied. *"Thanks, Jorge. Looks like a knife was used to sketch out a star on her chest by connecting the stab wounds."*

Jorge added, *"ugh, she drowned. Her lungs were filled with soapy water."*

A trail of bloody footprints came from the tiled bathroom floor and on to the carpeted bedroom floor. The second victim was a white male, found naked and face down on the floor with blood on his chest and arms. A bloody knife encircled with yellow tape rested inches from his left hand. This victim was approximately fifty-five years old, about six feet tall, weighed roughly 200 pounds. The man had severe trauma to the right side of the head, but other than the head trauma, there was no other injury on his body.

Diego looked around the bedroom, smelling his way into the bedroom following the aroma of roses. He found a bouquet of red roses on a night table near the bed. A card attached to the dozen roses read, "Love thy self, Cecilia!" In the bathroom, he opened a sliding mirrored door to the closet. The closet smelled heavy with burnt wax and incense. Inside, he found a small altar, containing a two-foot sculpture made out of Chinese characters with melted wax dripping down its front side; eight partly burned red roses lay in front of the sculpture; and two newspaper articles cut-outs from the San Francisco Chronicle, placed side by side in front of the altar. At the base of the altar, eleven garlic heads were displayed in two rows of five with a single garlic head on top of the second row. The physics of the arrangement of the offerings seemed rushed; the objects were unevenly spaced, as someone had built it in a hurry.

Diego scanned the newspaper articles concerning females murdered by their male escorts at five-star hotels in the San Francisco Bay area, including the Fairmont and the Ritz-Carlton.

All of them had been stabbed multiple times and left to bleed to death in bathtubs.

Diego remembered hearing about this serial killer, still at large, staying ahead of San Francisco City Police Department investigators, frustrating everyone, and frightening the general public. *"Was this woman another of his unfortunate victims? But, if so, who is this man?"* Diego asked himself.

Perhaps the man lying on the floor was the Five-Star Hotel Killer?

Serial killers often leave their signature: knife wounds to the chest, a confession, or a letter. Was the altar his signature?

The Captain, too, entertained the remote possibility that the woman had been murdered by the Five-Star Hotel killer, but he did not want to voice that suspicion until the investigation had ruled out the most likely type of suspect—a jealous ex-husband or lover, who would definitely have a motive to kill the man she was with, and possibly her, as well.

Pointing to the dead man on the floor, Captain Williams asked: *"Could this man have raped and killed the female victim,"* he asked, raising his pointed finger, and holding his arm straight, pointed towards the bathroom, *"and then walked from the bathroom to the bedroom, where he was surprised by an intruder and sustained a blow to the head, right here by the front of the bed? Or did a different perpetrator kill both victims?"*

"Most murderers don't leave altars," Diego said. *"We can't ignore that. I can find out, but I've never read anything about an altar at the Five-Star Hotel killer crime scenes."*

The police used two conference rooms in the hotel to interview Claremont Hotel staff. They quickly learned that the female victim was Dr. Cecilia Rollins, a club member who was recently widowed. Mrs. Rollins had reserved the room for two weeks. She had been observed eating in one of the hotel's restaurants on several occasions with different young white males. She had also been seen lingering over a cocktail in the Paragon bar with a young handsome Asian male. Police interviewed the cleaning woman, who said she had not seen anyone in the room when she cleaned it at 11 that morning. The female victim had played tennis at noon and had a massage afterwards. Stanley Marconi, the tennis pro and exercise instructor said he had cautioned Dr. Rollins about using male escort services in the past. The masseuse, a Marilyn Hastings, said nothing seemed unusual, other than her client seemed in a hurry, as she said she had a date at 5 pm. A room service waiter reported that at 6:30 pm, he delivered dinner for two, with two bottles of red wine, to the room, and Dr. Rollins gave him a big smile and a generous tip. That was apparently the last time anyone saw her alive.

Captain Williams ordered the investigators to request telephone records for Dr. Rollins and to search her browsing history and other computer files on the laptop found in the room. Two ambulances came and took the dead bodies to the coroners. The white male victim did not appear to have been registered at the hotel; neither had anyone seen him in the hotel or at the club. The police ended their interrogation of the staff, and as soon as they had cleared out from the hotel grounds, the hotel resumed its former elegance as if nothing had occurred.

At the Berkeley Police Department on Martin Luther King Jr. Way, the Homicide Division was humming like a beehive: pictures of the crime scene were enlarged, tacked to bulletin boards and arrows drawn to indicate relevant evidence. After they had explored the different scenarios and possible theories about the Claremont Hotel killings, investigators were left with one unlikely, but intriguing possibility, that the dead man was the Five Star Hotel Killer. This theory was bolstered when Captain Williams picked up the telephone, and after a brief conversation, announced that forensics had just confirmed that the white male victim's fingerprints matched those found at the scenes of two of the other Five-Star Hotel homicides.

But if the white male was the Five Star Hotel Killer, how did he meet his death? Who had killed him? There was no forensic evidence of another person in the room.

The detectives speculated that an unknown killer made the altar after murdering the Five Star Hotel Killer, concluding that the altar was probably not created by Five Star Hotel Killer, but instead by someone who targeted the Five Star Killer.

The briefing took over an hour before reaching consensus; the Five Star Hotel Killer had murdered his seventh victim and died from trauma to the head inflicted by a third person. Finally everyone went their separate ways to further study the case and to work on other pending cases of the Berkeley Police Department. Diego walked into his office and logged onto the police files from various Bay area jurisdictions. Checking with an investigator friend with the San Francisco PD, Diego learned that newspaper clippings on the previous Five Star murders did not have altars on the list of evidence, thus he concluded that someone other than the Five Star Killer left the alter at the Claremont Hotel. What in the world was going on? He keyed in killings that shared common evidence; women murdered with a knife, women found dead in bathtubs, alters, candles, Chinese sculptures, and roses, dating back fifty years. He got hundreds of hits. Now he just had to look through them. The time flew by and many people left the building before Diego noticed that Captain Williams and he were the only ones left in the homicide division. Diego waved at the Captain as he walked by his office on his way out.

The police release read, *Double homicide at Claremont Hotel in Oakland, California: White female drowns in bathtub and white male dies from severe trauma to the head.*

On Diego's way home, he turned right on University Avenue and left on Shattuck Avenue towards the guest house where he temporarily lived while he guarded the house of a world renowned physicist living under police protection, which Diego provided during the night shift. The main house had a wall around most of the property and a huge adobe entrance with an iron gate. The remote gate opened swiftly for Diego. He drove into a private garage and walked into his living quarters. Even though the guest quarters were initially meant for the caretakers, it had a breathtaking view of the bay.

Diego walked by the laundry room, took off his clothes and jump shot his socks and underwear into the laundry basket. He put on his casual clothes, opened a bottle of red wine, and sat by the computer. Since Diego didn't have a love interest, and rarely dated; he spent most of his so-called free time on the job, solving homicides. He had always had a "feel" for solving cases, mysteries, and puzzles. Ever since he was a child, he wanted to be a detective. He loved his job and he was married to it. Again, he did an Internet search for homicides with similar evidence as found at the Claremont Hotel. Some hits, he had not seen at work.

First he grouped the links into folders: male and female victims, altars, candles, newspaper articles, roses, and the use of a knife as the murder weapon. Because Dr. Rollins had used an Internet escort service, he focused on the oldest profession, since it has always walked the streets on the wild side and sleeps with death too often. The computer screen displayed a map of the Bay Area with red pins tacked into it depicting the number of women killed over the last fifty years.

He found a case in Chinatown, which involved a homicide of a Chinese man, where an elaborate altar was decorated and a funerary urn designed out of Chinese characters was partly burned. Candles of all sizes littered the altar and newspaper clippings were scattered in front of the candles. The newspaper articles described the murders of Chinese transvestites: they were strangled, sodomized, and penis surgically removed. Diego was mystified: eight roses were found placed on the altars at the Chinatown and the Claremont homicides. Now the police department had two homicides where roses were found on an altar. The Claremont homicide was becoming more complex than anyone had initially surmised. Detectives sorted and filed details of each homicide in their minds to hopefully some day close some of these unsolved homicides. Diego eagerly memorized many of the details of these cases with the determination to find a single thread directly connecting these murders to one killer: just one single thread.

Diego was glued to his laptop and the hours passed too quickly. Finally, by two in the morning, he had narrowed the investigation to twenty cases. Some cases had roses but not newspaper articles and others had evidence unrelated to the homicide, publications such as brochures of resorts, festivals, and annual celebrations; Día de los Muertos, Chinese's New Year, and Wine Tastings.

The research data cluttered his mind with endless possibilities. Faceless killers floated in and out of his dreams.

"*What do you look like?* " he screamed. Diego fought to wake up at this point in his dream. Some knowledge of the Claremont Hotel homicide had surfaced in his unconscious. He wanted to capture the thought before it moved on to the sea of thoughts, where fishing it out was nearly impossible.

"Serial killers want to get caught, yes!"

They want to be stopped because they know that they cannot stop themselves from killing again and again. The Alphabet Killer whose victims first and last names started with the same letter of the alphabet was never caught. He was smarter than the police. The Zodiac Killer and Jack the Ripper wrote to the police and left evidence in the form of their killer's signatures: strangulation or mutilations. Most serial killers have targets; children or mainly boys; prostitutes, or women. The type of target they choose is also a part of their signature.

The evidence from the Claremont Hotel homicide flashed through his mind, as he once again fell asleep: the altars and their offerings, pictures from the newspaper clippings, small and large candles flickered, a

Chinese sculpture burned, eight roses and garlic heads.........there it was! It's was the roses!

Chapter 5

Mi Casa es su Casa

Everyone is born to either live the life of a king, a queen, a beggar, a gardener, or a saint. Diego's mother Rosario, or as she was called, Doña Ro, was chosen to be a saint. She always saw the good in people and was not one to judge when her advice was sought out by the troubled many. Eventually, every farmworker living in the Conejeras ended up at her door, asking for guidance or simply seeking someone to listen to their life's troubles. Some people find out later in life what role they have to play in the scheme of things, but that was not the case for Rosario. It seems that Diego's grandparents knew her path when they named her Rosario. Perhaps being named after a sequence of prayers and a string of prayer beads bound her to prayer. Everyone who visited her house bowed when they entered the room, and the men and women kissed her right hand, the hand that she used to make the sign of the cross. *"En el nombre del padre, del hijo, y el Espiritú Santo."* She kissed her thumb knuckle and blessed the visitor: *"Vaya con Dios,"* prayed Rosario. The dreary and the distraught smiled when they saw her. Rosario had a presence and radiance that brightened people's days.

When she said *"mi casa es su casa,"* she meant it, and the invitation extended well beyond the physical house, to her body and spirit. Rosario freely gave of herself to her family and friends, and also to strangers. There was never any expectation on her part that the recipient of her generosity would return the favor. Rarely would you see her exhausted and when you did, she'd simply disappear for a brief siesta, reappear fresh, rested enough to take the weight of the world on her shoulders. Rosario was always in constant motion, doing some kind of work. Sometimes she could be seen hunched over the stove, momentarily still as if in prayer, then she would continue working. It didn't matter how tired she was, she was able to work up a smile for you. She had the ability to look deeply into their souls with her penetrating dark brown eyes. One look, and she knew their pain. No one ever claimed Doña Ro talked with God, but they knew she had a divine connection. Every night, without fail, and when she first arose, Rosario was on her knees, praying. She believed in Jesús, our Savior, and entrusted her life to his safekeeping.

The thought of birth control did not enter her mind, so childbearing and raising her children provided the rhythm and foundation in her life. First came Roberto, followed by María and José, two stillbirths and then Carmela, Rosie, Gilberto, Diego, and Socorro.

Diego saw Rosario as a devoted mother, who loved each and every one of her eight children dearly. She'd make sure that they were fed, had clean clothes to wear, and like the best detective, she always knew the exact whereabouts of her children. Everyone hugged and kissed her on the hands and face. Don Robo didn't kiss her hand, although he often kissed her on the lips in public. He demonstrated in so many ways that he ruled over his family, just as he did over his workers: not going to church with his family, staying late any day he wanted, and sometimes not coming home for days. Rosario continued to request that he attend church with no results. Don Robo did relent and agree to drive the family to and from the Catholic Church. Although Don Robo never implied he was scared to step inside the church, his words and behavior told Diego otherwise: he thought that his father had sinned too much to step inside a church, at least not while he was alive. He often said, *"The only way you'll see me in church is in a wooden box,"* with a laugh. Diego was not convinced that his father thought it was funny. The expression of uncertainty in Don Robo's eyes didn't match his words.

Diego's house seemed to always have people traveling through it, as his mother considered everyone to be one extended family. His mother was so widely known and respected that even father Gregorio kissed her hand on the steps of the church, in front of the Anglo community and God. On Sundays, Rosario beamed with contentment and outright joy, her family and friends gathered around her on the steps of the church.

It is often said that God does not hand out more than one can handle, but to any observer, Rosario's burden seemed heavier than most. On her shoulders, she carried the burden of the family and all the conejitos living in the Conejeras. No sooner than one important social event would come to a successful end, right smack middle of everything would be Doña Ro orchestrating the distribution of labor for the next one. She gave out the marching orders, everyone fell into line and the event took place. Don Robo brought order to the farmworkers in the fields and Doña Ro brought order to the Conejeras. How could one woman do so much? Everyone wondered where she found so the energy and love to give it away so freely.

After church, Doña Ro routinely washed the clothes for the week to come. While checking the pants pockets, Rosario learned a great deal about each of her children and husband. From the stains and smell of the clothes, she found out when each of the girls had begun their menstrual cycle and when they had been with a man. As it turns out, it was the muddy knees on Diego's jeans and a mother's keen sense of observation, which led to the discovery of the "Foxhole." With her limited English, she convinced the ice cream company manager to fill in the "hole and tunnels" in their empty lot. *"¡Peligroso!"* she exclaimed, thrusting her arms up in the air. *"Not safe, people die!"* The manager, already dealing with a disability claim from an injured worker; he rented a tractor, hauled in some dirt and leveled the field.

The timing of Doña's Ro interventions with the troubled souls seemed to instill her with spiritual fortitude. Those residents who lived within the confines of the Conejeras had already encountered Doña Ro's expectations as to their roles in la familia. The women and girls acquired the ability to know when Doña Ro wanted, needed, or expected them to work for the benefit of la familia. No matter what was it they were doing at the time, they'd momentarily held their heads still and connected with the realization that they needed to attend to a family matter, and provide a service to the Conejera community. As Doña Ro respected them, they returned the devotion ten-fold with reverence and fellowship.

It was a special day, because *un chisme*, an unconfirmed rumor, had been circulating through the Conejeras that Don Robo was negotiating a year-round contract for most of the workers who traveled with him from México to Oregon. Anticipation was sky-high. This would mean everything to the workers, as their families would be able to stay in one place, and have a reason for them to truly say "mi casa es su casa."

"Rosario!" called Doña Ro's sister, Cristina. *"Where do you want me to put the pozole?"* The counter and kitchen tables were crowded with plates and pots of Mexican food. Some people knocked before entering the house, other just walked in, dropped the food somewhere and left to get dressed for the fiesta.

Since Cristina learned to cook pozole, she was always asked to cook delicious pozole for every gathering. The mixture of chiles, onions, and garlic filled the air with a pungent, spicy aroma. Tommy, Doña Ro's special friend, brought the best chile verde cooked in the Conejeras. Chile verde was his signature dish. All the people who tasted the pozole loved it, but they didn't always choose pozole. They did, however, serve themselves some chile verde. Tommy's chili verde had been elevated to the heights of the classic staple, *frijoles*. Chile verde was good at any time of the day. Yes, even at breakfast, with huevos rancheros floating in chili verde salsa. Doña Ro made sure that everyone ate well, even the single men living in the two conejeras.

"Diego," called Carlos. *"Rosa sends six dozen tamales for la primera cena to commemorate the start of la Cosecha, the harvest season."* Carlos held his arms out with three dozen hanging from each hand. Carlitos was bigger and stronger than most boys his age. He could hold a plastic bag with three-dozen tamales with each stretched-out arm with ease.. Cristina walked up to the table and pushed aside a large pot of rice resting on a ceramic square and Carlos piled the six bags of tamales on top of one another. Carlos looked around and

didn't see Diego and not wanting to be in a roomful of strangers, left. The bed and partitions were broken-down, folded and moved to one side of the room and a table was placed in the center. To serve as chairs and benches, they scattered suitcases and wooden boxes around the room. A painted wooden statue of La Virgén de Guadalupe blessed the food. The table was set for a festive primera cena, the first supper. Don Robo was expected within an hour and then everyone could sit down and eat.

Doña Ro's third child, José took charge of making Jamaica, a tangy, sweet tea made from the crimson petals of the Hibiscus flower, along with lemonade and coffee. Carmela and Rosie made tortillas all morning: large flour ones and three different sizes of corn tortillas for taquítos, tostadas, and enchiladas.

Don Robo was due to arrive, but the time came and it passed. Two hours later, most of the guests had returned to the Conejeras and awaited the invitation to eat. José, who ran track for the Gilroy High School cross-country team, jogged to the railroad crossing on Tenth Street. Once there, he quickly noticed that a stalled train had blocked passage and traffic had backed up on both sides of the tracks. He ducked under a railroad car, and crossed to the other side.

"*¿Que pasa?*" he asked two men who seemed to be arguing.

"*El pinche tren se Chingo,*" a man swore at the stalled train.

"*Yeah, the pendejo engineer broke the train. Now it does not start,*" interrupted the second and continued arguing.

The traffic jam stretched as far as he could see. José whistled his *cucuy* call, hoping Don Robo could hear it and return the call. After several whistles, he gave up. He did not hear a return whistle from Don Robo. The traffic jam got worse and the people more frustrated: horns honked, people cussed at each other, blaming each other for the calamity.

40

"*Traffic is jammed on both sides of the railroad tracks on Tenth Street and probably on other crossings as well. The train is not moving,*" José reported to Doña Ro.

She wondered if Don Robo was stuck in the traffic jam, still negotiating a labor contract or whether he would not come home at all, as he'd done so many times before. On the third hour, Rosario decided to let the hungry people eat. She knew that she was taking a risk of inviting violence. At least twice a year, Don Robo would cause such a scene that almost always someone was badly hurt. *People have to eat*, thought Rosario. She put out the word to re-invite the conejitos to our conejera for a meal.

The smell of fresh cut cilantro and onions for the Pico de Gallo and soups meant that they were about to be served. Most of the food could be kept warm or even reheated, but the Pico de Gallo had to be fresh and sweet to the palate.

Rosario waited until the room filled with friends and family before she blessed the meal and all who had prepared it, and thanked the Lord for the health of her family and friends, "*Nuestro bendito Dios, gracias por la salud de nuestra familia y amigos, tambien gracias a Dios por esta comida que fué preparada por todos en la familia.*" She added a prayer that the negotiations would go well. "*Espero que todo va bien con los negocios de Don Robo.*" Rosario made the sign of the cross.

"*Amen,*" they all followed.

First, the elders were served and sat comfortably at their place of choice. The men followed in honor of their hard work. The women and young girls helped with the children next before sitting down to eat.

The talking quieted down as they ate their first bites of food. While they chewed their favorite food, without exception they all wondered what had happened to Don Robo.

"*Why was he so late?*'

Chapter 6

Altar Offerings

Since the beginning of the human race, further back than the Paleolithic era, man has constructed altars at funeral sites in an attempt to communicate with the spiritual world. Through time, the dead have been buried in the ground with a single cross above the grave, or in a tomb with sculptured decorations, as in the Sarcophagi of the Constantine Epoch where the body rests in peace and the spirit leaves the body a little bit at a time, or the opposite, as in the instantaneous departure, a launch into space by Pakal, a Mayan leader who is etched on a stone sarcophagus in the Temple of Inscriptions Pyramid in Palenque, México. In prayer and in song, the gods are invoked to accompany the dead into the spirit world. A burial site, an urn full of the dead man's ashes, or an empty sarcophagus serves as a reminder of the journey's origin. From this ending, or new beginning, the dead can return home and refuel with the food and sweet bread left on the altar and find a sense of home in his photographs decorating the altar.

Diego was no stranger to the ritual of building altars. As a child he participated in many Día de los Muertos celebrations, where he learned about his grandparents, great grandparents and great-great grandparents from old pictures that reappeared in November of each year. Diego placed empanadas de calabaza, turnovers made of pumpkin, and pan dulce with pink and yellow toppings to the left of the La Virgén de Guadalupe. "The dead must be fed," he prayed silently. He and his childhood friend Carlos had also built altars in their hideouts: great places for storing secret treasures like weapons and food.

Back at the office the next morning, Diego continued to studying old files, looking for some link that would implicate a third person of the Five Star Hotel homicides.

As Diego studied each file, he found other unsolved homicides that had altars, newspaper articles and roses. In a case, which occurred in San Francisco's Chinatown, the victim was a killer who targeted transvestites. According to the evidence he reviewed, the crime scene; a burned Chinese sculptured candle with multiple wicks protruding from the structure. The sculpture was designed in such a way that all the wicks could be lit with one match. Diego felt a warm rush travel through his body and his face flushed with blood speeding to the brain— another connection.

Diego shared his conclusions with the captain and his colleagues on the investigation team. "I've found two cases, one in Chinatown and another in Gilroy that contain similar evidence as those found at the Claremont Hotel homicides. All three had altars with roses, an intricate Chinese candle, and newspaper clippings implicating the murdered victim as a person of interest." He went on: "In the case of the Gilroy homicide, the murder took place in a closed-up tent at the Garlic Festival. The victim was a wealthy farmer. It had an altar, too, with 6 roses on it. The crime scene also included an unlit candelabra made out of Chinese characters, and a small Christ child statue. At all three homicides, the altar and offerings were strategically placed on a red satin cloth." The team studied the evidence from the cases and reached a consensus that there were too many striking connections between these three cases for it to be a coincidence.

Still, Captain Williams was cautious with making connections between the three cases. In light of the homicides at the Garlic Festival and Chinatown, the captain partnered a Hispanic and a Chinese detective to the Rose Cases. The door opened and in entered a young Chinese woman, dressed in slacks and a matching light brown blazer; a ponytail used to play down her attractive features. The Captain introduced Diego to his new partner on the Claremont Hotel Homicide Case. "Detective Chi Ling, formerly from Oakland Police Department, this is detective Diego de Campos. Now, you two, head on out to San Francisco and see what you can find out on this Roses Case."

Chi listened attentively to the Captain, shook hands with Diego and followed him to the car pool. "Diego, I'm glad to have the opportunity to work with you on these cases."

"The feeling is *mutual*, Detective Ling," smiled Diego as he drove towards San Francisco.

Coincidentally, the San Francisco Police Department had named the Chinatown homicide "the Eight Roses Case." The same number of roses was found on the altar as were found at the Claremont Hotel case. These two cases were eerily similar, other than the fact that the newspaper clippings found at each scene implicated different homicide victims, both of them suspects in earlier murders. From this point on, Diego referred to the cases by the number of roses left on the altar: the Chinatown case was named 8 Roses Number One, the Claremont case as 8 Roses Number Two. In the San Francisco case, the murder victim was a white male in his fifties, weighing about two hundred ten pounds. It appeared that he was killed at his own home. The newspaper articles described the murders of three Chinese transvestites over the past two years. Each had their penis removed with a surgical knife.

Witnesses had seen a man dressed in black leaving the house and running down the alley. The man in black was described as six feet tall and a fast runner. The pictures of the victim showed him face down in his living room floor. He had died from trauma to the head—the same cause of death as 8 Roses Number Two. Forensics found only the victim's fingerprints and DNA in the room. In both cases, the police could not establish how the victims had sustained such a lethal blow to the head, and the perpetrator did not leave any evidence at the crime scene.

Chi Ling intently studied the evidence from both crime scenes. She made photocopies of the photos of the Chinese character statues, cut out the burnt parts of the two characters, and made one Chinese character out of them. A smile blossomed through her face, "Diego, look!" Diego studied the Chinese character, and then looked at her, puzzled. "It reads, 'Rose' in Chinese," added Chi. "That has to be an important clue," she said. Diego felt a chill moving through his body. He was right about the roses.

Back in the office, the two reported: "Captain, in the 8 Roses case in San Francisco five years ago, the candelabra included Chinese characters spell the word 'Rose.' The one in Gilroy, which happened ten years earlier, also had the same Chinese characters. Plus, six red roses were left on the altar, very similar to our 8 Roses case at the Claremont" reported Diego, while he looked at Chi, expecting her to jump in and tell the story in her own words, to describe how she discovered that the Chinese characters on the candelabra must have some kind of symbolic importance. To Chi, credit belonged to the team and not to the individual.

A filing clerk in the briefing room corrected Diego's assessment. "Diego, you keep referring to the Claremont Hotel homicide as the 8 Roses Case, well not counting the dozen red roses found in the bedroom because they were not actually found on the altar, two other slightly burnt red roses were found on the carpet in the bedroom. There were a total of ten, not eight roses found on the altar at Claremont Hotel homicides," added the clerk.

"Diego your hunch is right on target," said Chi proudly. While she never accepted credit for herself, she was always the first one to give credit when someone else earned it. "You said that every serial killer leaves his signature at the crime scene so that he can get credit for the homicide. He is using the altar to communicate with us. Everything on the altar has a meaning," she continued with the enthusiasm of having made a discovery. 'If these cases are connected, as they certainly appear to be, the roses tell us the sequence of his killings," Chi smiled at Diego, making him uncomfortable with the attention.

"Yeah! Chi, let's follow the roses in sequential order. Here is what we have: the first case we know about is the 6 Roses Case. It happened fifteen years ago in Gilroy and about five years ago, the 8 Roses Case in Chinatown and now we have the 10 Roses Case at the Claremont Hotel,"

The Captain jumped in and yelled at his administrative assistant from across the room, "Sharon, prepare a news release."

"What should it read?" cried Sharon with a frustrated look, since she was not involved in the briefing, even though she was in the same room. She went back to her computer and addressed the email with the release protocols and waited for the Captain, who was highly stressed because at the moment, he was handling two new homicides that may have been committed by the same serial killer, not to mention a bombing at a school and a bank robbery.

The room of the double homicide at the Claremont Hotel in Berkeley was registered to victim number one, Dr. Cecelia Rollins, a member of their health club and a frequent guest. Berkeley Police Department has not produced the identity of the male victim, although Captain Williams reports that partial fingerprints match those found at two of the other Five Star Hotel homicides in the Bay Area.

The Captain, as a veteran police officer, knew that he could not afford to be too impressed with the amount of progress made on the Claremont Hotel case, because the trail could go cold just as fast. He directed Diego and Chi to visit the Gilroy Police Department. Chi and Diego drove south on Highway 101 and were at the Gilroy Police Office before the lunch hour. The two detectives on the case were about to leave for lunch when they were asked to remain behind to assist the detectives from the Berkeley Police Department.

The data files of unsolved cases similar to the Garlic Festival homicide (6 Roses Case) were taken in a conference room and placed on a table in the middle of the room. The fourth wall faced the hallway was all windows. After brief formalities, the four detectives dove into the evidence, all with the same mindset. The two Gilroy officers opened up the folders and Diego and Chi separated photographs and evidence. Fidel Costa, one of the Gilroy police officers, wrote the names of the pieces of evidence on the whiteboard as Diego dictated them: Altars, red satin cover, Chinese character, and roses.

With all the excitement, Diego and Chi took turns asking questions in rapid fire, "What condition were the roses in when they were found? Fresh, wilted, or were they dry and stiff? Were they in a bundle, spread out, or in a vase?"

"Please understand that we do not mean to sound intrusive, but we have a serial killer on the loose and right now the trail is hot," contributed Chi in an apologetic manner.

"The roses were separated about six inches from each other, as if they should be individually admired," Fidel pointed out. "A postcard of the Santa Cruz boardwalk was found at the foot of the altar," he said, as if the postcard was evidence from another unsolved case.

Chi instinctively knew that the tourist brochure, the eleven garlic heads found at the Claremont murder, and the postcard of the boardwalk were somehow connected. "She asked herself: "What is the connection?"

"What is your name, again?" asked Diego.

"Daniel Hustler," replied the officer.

"Well, Daniel, can you get permission to call the Santa Cruz Police Department and ask if they have any more unsolved homicides containing the similar evidence outlined on this board? Have them go back at least ten years!" Daniel took notes and left the conference room.

Minutes later Daniel came back with an email from the Santa Cruz Police Department reporting on a homicide that took place more than ten years ago: the evidence included a red satin matt with a Chinese funerary structure on it, candles, seven roses, and an incense burner boat. The Boardwalk case had not come up before in Diego's search because the police report had not described the layout of the evidence as an altar. The email had an attachment of a picture of six yellow roses carefully placed two inches apart.

"OK!" exclaimed Chi. "Now we are getting somewhere. At the Garlic Festival fifteen years ago, we have the 6 Roses case, four years later, 7 Roses happens in Santa Cruz at the Boardwalk, and three years after that, the 8 Roses case happens in Chinatown. The evidence that pointed to the Santa Cruz Boardwalk homicide was a postcard found at the 6 Roses Case. What in the 8 Roses case can point to the possible location of the next murder? Where is the clue that points to 9 Roses?" Chi wondered.

"The newspaper clipping that we found at the Boardwalk homicide implicated the murdered man as a suspect child molester. Two of the children he was alleged to have molested committed suicide. Another boy he was related to died after beomg brutally sodomized. Even though there was never enough evidence to convict him on any of those cases, everyone thought he was guilty of all three crimes. A real sicko!" explained Daniel.

Officer Castro said, "Wait a minute." He left the conference room and returned with notes from the file and noted that a brochure of the Dickens' Faire was found at the crime scene. "I took these notes when I reviewed the evidence from the 8 Roses Case file," he added. "I just thought about it because I wanted to take my children to the Dickens' Faire in San Francisco this Christmas. It was found on a table in the tent where the murder occurred, but I had no idea it could be important evidence." he said.

Diego and Chi were smiling at each other as if they had swallowed a canary. "All of this seems to be pointing us in the direction of the case that most likely occurred between the Gilroy case and the Claremont case, which we can assume was the 9 Roses Case." They shared their suspicions with the officers and their thought that this clue might represent a potential "break" in the case and within ten minutes Chi and Diego were back on Highway 101 heading north. Chi called the San Francisco Police Department to determine which of the four police stations should Diego drive to further investigate the 9 Roses Case.

"Chi, call the Captain and asked him if he has any problem with us going into San Francisco to investigate a potential lead to 9 Roses Case" directed Diego. Chi had started to dial the Captain before Diego had asked her to make the call.

The San Francisco daily rush hour was about to start.

Chapter 7

"Aquí Yo Mando!"

Here, I Rule!

Roberto de Campos has no memory of his father, Manolo. He abandoned the family and took off for El Norte after his mother, Remedio, gave birth to the eighth child. Roberto was a year and two months old when his father left their hometown, Saltillo, México for the United States. Acutely feeling his father's absence, Roberto attached himself to his mother. Being around her, he learned the art of family management. His mother ran an efficient labor force that kept the family in constant motion. Like all mothers, she was the caretaker, the center of all activity. Roberto learned to cook and how to prepare for cultural events, family activities, birthday celebrations, El Día de los Muertos, and selected saint's day observances. The children's favorite celebration was All Saints day. The skill to mobilize a family for an event is a gift, and it takes experience, proper training and collaboration skills. Roberto certainly received daily training, but it was already his natural inclination to command: to rule and have the final word on business matters.

"*Ya lo dije!*" he would say, "I said it, and I mean it." He would give the order and the work would be done.

By the time Roberto was 19 years of age, he practically ruled the family; his older brothers, sisters, and even his mother took orders from him without hesitation or resentment. All the time he spent in the kitchen gave him some authority to hold up the palote, the roller for making tortillas, and wheel it around in circles. His mother had to occasionally remind him that her chancla, the sandals she used to paddle the children, ruled over his palote.

Roberto took over the reins of the family not because he was a bully, although he later became one, but because somebody had to and he was the best prepared. When Remedio developed a heart condition, her tired body moved about with difficulty. Roberto stepped right in and to took command. He moved quickly, as if he had been prepared for this purpose; he ordained himself as the one to be listened to.

"*Aquí yo mando,*" he proclaimed. *"I'm in charge."*

At his twenty-first birthday, a fiesta declared Roberto, *El Grande*. His grandfather on his father's side of the family was known as El Grande, which was a power status accorded to only a few men in each generation of the de Campos lineage. Roberto, not wanting anything to remind him of his father, adopted a new name, Don Robo. At first, his brothers, sisters, mother, and friends were grateful for his leadership, but through the years and the rough times, Roberto evolved into a different person, certainly very different than the one who spent his mornings at his mother's side.

After Remedio had a stroke, she lost her will to live. She was a prisoner inside a lifeless body. She had once been the ruler of her kitchen, a force to be reckoned with. She was bedridden for a year before she passed. As she requested, she was buried behind the adobe house, next to the mesquite tree with no fanfare or prayer. The brothers and sisters circled the grave and stood motionless as if petrified like the rocks at Stonehenge that are aligned with the stars. Later that day before darkness, each of her children took some time to be alone with Remedio.

Roberto walked up to the mesquite. He was a man with no father and now no mother, an orphan. The struggle to provide for a family of eight was daunting and it left no time for pleasure or entertainment. Five years of ruling over a family of seven teenagers was more than he could take any longer. He talked to his mother, at her gravesite, *"We are going to "El Norte, we must leave our beloved Saltillo, México, our birth place and follow the North Star."*

*   *   *   *

He had brought his family and they waited under the pecan trees at the outskirts of town. Don Robo negotiated the crossing of la frontera into Texas. Everything was so well arranged that in twenty-four hours, they were already working. They now had an opportunity to dream beyond the rancho. Don Robo traded their

55

labor for passage; without cash up front, the *coyote*, a human trafficker, charged double the price for passage. As always, the coyote behaved consistent with his nature, which was to take advantage of helpless and vulnerable undocumented workers.

The coyote was a great teacher to Don Robo. With each deal he learned more and acquired more authority. By the second migrant labor campaign, accompanying by his new wife, Rosario, the de Campos family had their own truck. The summer months filled the rural landscape with Mexican farm workers. Among the network of farm workers, Don Robo had a caravan of five trucks following him in a much larger network of farm workers. The ranchers preferred dealing with contractors rather than with each individual family. Don Robo called many farmers by their first names, and they all called him Don Robo. Around the farmers, Don Robo spoke English with a Spanish accent, but around his family he spoke Spanish. The farmers felt superior to Don Robo, yet somehow Don Robo negotiated good contracts for his workers. They were paid well, but they sometimes felt like beasts of burden, especially when they had to work long hours, complete a contract and move to the next farm. None of the workers were allowed to get close to anyone in the farmers' families. They worked and parted before any relationship or friendship could take root. The migrant families moved into a community, stayed in the marginal labor camps and left after the harvest.

Don Robo did not like being challenged by his workers. His motto was, he found the work and the workers worked. It was that simple. He did not have to argue or fight with his workers because if they did not like his orders, they were replaced with another family. On one occasion, Don Robo did fight his cousin, Pepé. He managed to hurt Don Robo right away with unblocked right crosses. As drunk as Don Robo was, he just kept coming, punch after punch. He just kept coming. That's one thing about fighting Don Robo; it was going to be a long fight, no matter what happened, somebody was going to get badly hurt. Even those trying to stop the fight could be hurt.

As time passed, Don Robo became meaner and meaner to his workers and even more distant with his family. He enjoyed the Friday and Saturday evenings in the local cantinas. The cantina was his castle, the place where he felt like a king and where he was treated with respect. After the sixth bottle of beer, Don Robo started buying rounds; before long, a fight would break out just because he needed to get rid of the anger that was eating away at him.

All that was needed to find a fight is to call out to someone in the bar, *"You Son of a Bitch! ¡Chinga tu madre, Hijo de la Chingada!"* Chairs levitated, beer bottles took flight, and boot heels ended up high in the air. Sometimes, a fight between two turned into a larger bar brawl. And it rarely stopped there. Those that didn't want to get knifed later avoided the alleys, instead selected to stay in the bar to get beat up in public.

*   *   *   *

During the week, Don Robo supervised work groups in three different farms, not affording him the time to pick fruit along with his workers. Although he was knowledgeable of farming and gardening, rarely would he have to demonstrate to workers how fast he wanted them to work and how to work together. His major goal was to manage the workers and to have the harvest hauled to the canneries. At one of the farms under his contract, his crew was completing the seasonal work when he learned that Mr. Michael Johnson, a farmer under contract, had passed and his widow, Mrs. Rebecca Johnson, was living there alone. Mr. Romano, the custodian of the family secrets, directed Don Robo to care for Mrs. Johnson's garden. Don Robo stopped by on several occasions to maintain the garden. One day, Mrs. Johnson came out to listen to the birds singing by her window. Don Robo was kneeling by a plant that he was replacing with a rose bush.

"Where are the birds? I hear birds singing!" she said aloud, not

noticing Don Robo.

"The birds you heard, well, that was I, whistling! Oh, Mrs. Johnson! I hope Mr. Ramano inform you that I would care for your garden," Don Robo apologized without an accent.

"Who are you?" asked Mrs. Johnson sternly.

"I am Don...," he started to introduce himself but used his first name with her, *" I am Roberto, your late husband's labor contractor."* he answered as he turned to face her.

"Oh! Thank you for helping me out with the garden, I wouldn't know what to do," she added timidly.

Under the gloomy face was a pretty one and Don Robo was struck right away. *"Please wait,"* he requested. He quickly went in the shed and came out with a pair of rubber garden cloves, hand rake, and short hoe. *"Slowly rake the sprouting weeds around the plants,"* he said with a smile.

"The whistling was nice!" whispered Mrs. Johnson; "people call me Becky!" lowered her head and feeling rather embarrassed to also use her first name.

Canaries, parrots, finches, and nightingales blessed the garden with their melodious songs. When Don Robo introduced each bird song, the volume was barely audible, but progressively the song grew louder until the type of bird was clearly evident: parrots, nightingale, finches, and pigeons took turns singing. He also loved to whistle some of his favorite Ranchera songs: "Aye, Aye, canto y no lloro!"

Mrs. Johnson loved the idea of gardening, something her husband never allowed her to do. She worked near her door and before she realized Don Robo was gone. By late afternoon the next day, there he was again working in the garden. He showed up for an hour almost every afternoon for two weeks before she offered him some food. *"Roberto, would you like to have a glass of wine and cheese with me."*

"*Sure,*" Robo exclaimed, taking off his sombrero, he was surprised by the invitation. Mrs. Johnson no longer had a face devoid of life and vitality; her face lifted as she smiled. Her gardener in a few minutes made her laugh. In the days that followed, she looked forward to gardening. The weeks passed with Don Robo making his frequent visits. He pointed out the different plants and gave them human characteristics: some were friendly, while others did not want to be disturbed. "*Rebecca, watch out for thorny people,*" he'd say to her. He described the plants in her garden as being friendlier than most people he knew. Rebecca laughed at the thought of plants having the characteristics of her family members. The neighbors and Mrs. Johnson's relatives began to be aware of Don Robo's work on her garden. For a woman who had not laughed in years, the neighbors muttered that it was odd to hear laughter coming from the Johnson's house.

Mr. Romano, who was known by just "Romano", owned more garlic and onion fields than anyone in the Gilroy area. The old man ordered Don Robo to care for the Johnson's property. On Romano's visits, he noticed Becky's friendly gestures to Don Robo while he worked in her garden. He voiced his suspicion that Don Robo was acting a little too familiar towards Becky. Her father-in-law, Edward Johnson, was also somewhat jealous that Don Robo visited her daily. It seems that the men had their eye on Rebecca Johnson.

During the contract negotiation for the year-round contract, Romano was meaning to give Don Robo a hard time and possibly kill the deal. He was sitting down when Don Robo entered the yard. Two other contractors were there to bid on the same contract. Having other labor contractors present was done to bring the price of labor down. Don Robo, knowing the scope of work and how many men and how many days it would take to do the work in the set timelines, negotiated the contract right out of everyone's reach. This, he was good at.

The other contractors chose to leave once the contract was given to Don Robo. Edward Johnson, Antonio Marconi, and

Romano had ordered snacks: cheeses, slices of French bread, olives, mixed fruits and a case of wine. Don Robo drank with them until he felt a little drunk. He heard Mr. Johnson confide to another man that *"the filthy spick"* was visiting his daughter-in-law and that he would kill him if he touched her.

The celebration was just another example of how the farmers treated farm workers; Don Robo had to fetch them drinks and food, even though it was a business celebration honoring the signing of the labor contract. In this setting, the farmers were the Patrónes and the farm workers were the peasants, and Don Robo was treated as a peasant. *"fetch me and John another glass of wine,"* he was ordered. Don Robo could feel that he was slightly drunk and he was afraid that if he didn't leave, he might feel compelled to fight one of them. As Don Robo left, he made sure they noticed that his English was as good as theirs.

"Gentlemen, it has been a pleasure to enter into a legal contract with respectable men like yourselves. Thank you for the wine and cheese party, but I have to leave. My family is waiting for word on this great opportunity to live in Gilroy twelve months out of the year."

Don Robo was a little late coming home that day. He drank wine with the bosses and by doing so possibly changed the family's way of life forever. Even so, he had mixed feelings about working for the same farmer year round. To a degree, he felt that he would lose some control of his workers. Oh, well at least the de Campos' no longer had to move. Don Robo hated the instability, the uncertainty and the packing and unpacking of the migratory life.

The traffic ahead was coming to a stop. After 5:30pm, all roads leading to and from his housing development were jammed. The parking lights of the vehicles ahead of him were flashing as cars inched along until they came to a complete stop. After waiting in the truck for fifteen minutes, he stepped out of the truck and observed that at least twenty vehicles in front of him and the cars behind him were beginning to form a long line. He stepped back in the truck and listened to the local radio station. One hour later and his eyes were bulging red with anger. The police began to reroute the traffic. On the turn, Don Robo learned that the train had some problems and that the traffic was blocked at the railroad crossing, separating Gilroy along the railroad tracks, and the train was not going to move anytime soon. Already more than two hours late, Don Robo finally found a country road where he could cross over the railroad tracks. He sped along the country roads and didn't slow down for the stop signs. He wasn't seeking death for himself, but someone needed to die for the embarrassment and shame that he had just experienced. He thought, *"don't they know that aquí yo mando, that I am the boss and not the servant?"*

"Voy a matar a alguien!" he wanted to get even, to kill someone.

When he drove into the Conejera's parking area in front of his house, there were no parking spaces. Someone had stopped by to deliver food, blocking Don Robo's parking space and were on their way out as he stepped into the house. He noted that everyone was already eating.

"Who gave the word to go ahead and eat? Who?" he shouted knowing the answer.

"¿¡Qué no saben que Aquí yo mando?!" he yelled loudly. Everyone stood like statues waiting for something to happen next. Suddenly, everyone moved away from Don Robo and raced towards the door, they scattered like cucarachas when the light is turned on.

Don Robo stepped up to the refrigerator, took out a carton of milk and drank from it, put it back, turned around and flipped over the table full of food, spluttering food on the walls and those that were close by were sprayed with Pico de Gallo and guacamole.

"You can't eat until I give the word," he screamed. *"¡Pórque! ¡Aquí yo mando!"*

Don Robo left after he changed his shirt, boots and put on his best hat. That night he made the rounds to drink at different bars looking for someone to fight. A tall gringo finally got mad at his loud mouth and fought him out in the alley behind the cantina. Don Robo was badly hurt, but he got up, brushed himself off, and went back to fight the gringo some more. Maybe those who looked on should have stopped the fight, but their lives were chiseled down to dust and left devoid of the backbone needed to stand for something.

The fights and the meanness that Don Robo exhibited to others was the result of not having anyone to counsel him about his problems. As he lay on the floor, bloodied, and cut, he whispered so that only he could hear, *"Why did you leave?"* The fights and self-inflicted punishment he brought on himself was still not as painful as the pain he felt from not having a father figure in his life.

Don Robo would return to his conejera badly injured and in need of medical care. Doña Ro nursed him as she always did, with a wet towel that she had dipped in cold water. She'd wipe the blood from his face and cover the deep cuts on his right cheek with lean ground beef patties. Don Robo woke up to a clean house, floors freshly mopped with Pine Sol. For a while, he behaved as if he was a model father and husband. A month or two later, Don Robo was back to his mean self, and hollering at the workers.

"¿Qué miran, pendejos?" he'd say when he caught someone looking at him with pity.

Chapter 8

Connecting the Dots

There, in the shadows, where the light is blocked by a tree and a building, the light angles away sharply and leaves a monster lurking in the dark, breathing hoarsely, spitting white of puffs of breathes upwards and seeing it dissipate into the light. This mind's eye lives daily in Dante's inferno along with the gargoyles and demons like him. A monster travels here and there with no identity or family. An uncontrollable anger resides beneath the surface of his skin: ready to erupt, and transform itself into another personality; killing on impulse, leaving evidence, his signature.

He is a serial killer because he is almost always in disguise; he is thoughtful, plans ahead- sometimes for years, and learns his victim's routine before he strikes the mortal blow. And while the life force of his victim leaves the body, the monster's rapture is amplified to such negative magnitudes that it is felt on the surface of the moon.

The natural forces that pull, push, and shape the souls and hearts of men are not without their Ying and Yang, Tezcatlipoca and Quetzalcoatl, or positive and negative. As the day surrenders to the night and the moon begins to reflect its artificial light, the monster steps into his host and onto the city streets.

*   *   *   *

A florist's truck parked at the entrance of the Omni Hotel in San Francisco. The driver dressed in a florist's uniform carried a large flower arrangement into the lobby. He wore a gray beret matching the color of the uniform. He had a thick beard and wore thick glasses. He slowly approached the front desk and announced, *"Roses for Dr. Rollins."* The attendant called for a porter to take the flowers from the florist. The attendant looked for Dr. Rollins' reservation. Just as the florist was able to hand over the flowers to the porter, the attendant said, "I am sorry, Dr. Rollins will not be staying at this hotel tonight."

"There must be a mistake, Dr. Rollins herself ordered the roses five days ago and insisted that we deliver the red roses today by 6:30 p.m. sharp," insisted the florist.

"You may leave them and we will places the red roses in her room," volunteered the receptionist.

"I am sorry, but Dr. Rollins explicitly said she wanted to personally receive them no later than 6:30pm," argued the florist.

"Well, she is registered, but left note that she was not staying tonight!" said the attendant with frustration and loud enough for other people standing around to hear.

"You may try the Claremont Hotel in Berkeley. She usually stays there when we are full," added the attendant who personally knew Dr. Rollins. She had called him to leave word concerning her secret rendezvous and of her stay at the Claremont Hotel, instead of the Omni Hotel.

"We are not privileged with the whereabouts of our members or our clientele," injected the first attendant with visible disapproval of the disclosure.

The florist appeared to be very upset, as his glasses seemed to fog with frustration and intolerance. He retrieved the bouquet of rose, did an about-face and walked hurriedly out of the hotel lobby, hopped in the truck and drove recklessly out of the hotel entrance. A car right behind the florist: raced out of the hotel exit in opposite direction and headed towards Berkeley. The florist raced through the heavy afternoon traffic and finally drove onto the Oakland Bay Bridge. The traffic moved slowly, the air filled with gas fumes and the roaring of engines that moved at a snail's pace.

The sun was setting; a fog was hovering over the Bay Bridge and the tall buildings along the way to the Oakland Hills. The hotel lobby at the Claremont Hotel was buzzing with the dinner rush. Two women dressed in formal gowns and four men in their tuxedos gathered by the front desk, asking for directions to the

Empire Ballroom where they were attending a wedding. The wall in the Empire Ballroom had high windows to showcase a spectacular view of the San Francisco skyline and the Golden Gate Bridge.

*   *   *   *   *

On the third floor of the Claremont, a maintenance man with latex gloves stepped out of the service elevator carrying black plastic bags and with a magnetic key entered Cecilia Rollins' room. As soon as the maintenance man entered the room, he knew he was too late. He heard the splashes in the bathtub; he set the bag down, and slipped on a black sweatshirt over his maintenance jacket, pulled the hood over his head veiling his face; blending into the darkness as he turned off the lights to the living room. He moved effortlessly from room to room turning off lights.

The killer sat in the bathtub embracing Dr. Rollin's limp body with his arms in bloody water. *"Rolling Stone, stop your rolling around in expensive hotels with men younger than your children,"* he said to her. He stroked her hair back with the bloody water. *"Sleep, go to sleep, Cecilia."*

The naked man looked up and towards the open door and noticed the lights go off in the bedroom. His bewildered stare pierced through the walls but he did not see anyone, but his monster's instincts detected the warmth from someone nearby. He reached out and grabbed the bloody knife he had placed at the base of the bathtub, pushed the woman's body aside from him and stepped out of the tub. Big splashes of water and blood followed him out of the tub. His wet footprints entered the bedroom. Standing with his back to the light and his face to the darkness of the room, he held the knife out, ready to strike. Taking a step forward, he extended his free hand, searching for the light switch along the wall.

At the same instant the lights were turned on, he was hit with a severe blow to the side of his head, short-circuiting his nervous system and dropping him where he stood. Once on the floor, blood oozed out of his ears and nose.

The door opened to an empty closet. A red mat was unrolled onto the second to the top shelf and a funerary structure with candlewicks sticking out from it was placed in the center. Smaller candles flagged both sides of the structure and ten red roses were carefully spaced out evenly on the red matt. Several of the wicks on the Chinese funerary structure and candles were lit. Newspaper articles of the 5 Star Hotel homicides were scattered along the floor in front of a makeshift altar. The man dressed in black closed the closet door, extinguishing the flames. Nonetheless, enough smoke filtered out through the cracks on the closet door that it activated the fire alarm.

The alarm was so loud that people came out of their rooms, running frantically to the exits. No one noticed the maintenance man walk out the front door and out on the parking lot.

*   *   *   *   *

Stanley Marconi, a former tennis pro, who now works part-time at the health club at the Claremont Hotel called from his mobile phone excitedly, *"Cecilia! I am back from Tuscany!"*

"Stanley, you fool. How can you twirl me around your little finger just like that, and expect me to change all my plans and come running to you?" argued Cecilia weakly.

"Well, do you have something better to do than play tennis with me?" he asked knowing very well that she would change her plans.

"I am bartending at a private Wine Tasting at the Claremont, near the Pool Arbor. It's sponsored by some of Santa Clara's wineries. It will be fun, lots of great wine with live music in the open air." The invitation

was irresistible to Cecilia. After her husband passed and now in her early fifties, she decided to fill her days with life's greatest gifts: frequent facials, exercise, massage, gourmet cuisine, wine tasting, and playing tennis with handsome young men. She had been committed to her husband even though he had been bedridden for the last ten years of his life. Certain that she did not want to remarry; she chose to enjoy the company of other men, outside her circle of friends and relatives.

Cecilia and Stanley had been good friends since they attended the same private Catholic high school. She was much like him: children whose wealthy parents left them in care of boarding schools managed by Catholic priests and nuns. Both from the same economic social class, they often found themselves at the same gatherings.

Stanley's life dream was to play professional tennis. He was definitely a talented tennis player, but he did not use performance drugs like most of the top ranked professional tennis players. Stanley had beaten some of top tennis players during non-tournament play, but the use of performance drugs was enough of an advantage that he consistently lost to them during tournament play. He was living his life's dream working at the Claremont Hotel Health Club and playing tennis any time he wanted.

"I am already scheduled to stay at the Omni for a week."

"Keep your reservations at Omni," he insisted. *"I will take care of booking you at the Claremont, we can hop between hotels for the week. OK!"*

With three taps on his I-Phone, Stanley made the changes to his world for at least the next two months, *"Siri! Call the Claremont Hotel, Club and Spa in Berkeley, California."*

"Claremont Hotel, Club and Spa reservations! How can I help you?" asked the attendant.

"*This is Stanley Marconi calling on behalf of Dr. Rollins,* " conveyed Stanley with confidence.

"*How can I help you, Stanley?*" asked the attendant.

"*Please make reservations for Dr. Rollins for the next two weeks in November,*" requested Stanley.

Yesterday Italy, today San Francisco, and for the two weeks at the Claremont Hotel with Cecilia, the two were living a fast life; unknowingly drowning in one giant martini.

*   *   *   *   *

Down a steep street in San Francisco, up a poorly lit stairway leading to a terraced restaurant with a small stage for performances to a fifty-person audience, you will find one of Chinatown's best-kept secrets. The heavy smokers kept the dining area in a heavy fog. Every table was full with prominent Chinese businessmen and beautiful Asian women. A huge Chinese man, known as the Dragon, sat quietly watching the performance of a beautifully dressed dancer who moaned and groaned her songs in a soft and melodious tune. The people sitting with the Dragon ate while the dancer sang and danced, but not the predator, he studied the movement of his next victim. The dancer moved ever-so-smoothly off the stage. Since the Dragon did not applaud at the end of the performance, no one else dared to.

The Dragon and his guests talked while they ate exotic gourmet food from plates and pots on the table. The servers stood motionless, waiting to immediately remove any used or unwanted dishware. The Dragon went out of his way to intimidate people and instill fear in the hearts of those that served him. When he finished eating, the others knew that they too had to stop eating. The servants swiftly cleared the table before disappearing behind the curtains. When the Dragon stood up, the others moved away from the doorway so that he could exit without any obstructions.

He entered the white limousine while it was running; the exhaust kept poisoning the air. The 'click n' clack' of the dancer's shoes followed as she stepped into the backseat of a limousine that drove into the grey fog of a dark night.

Inside the limousine, the Dragon and the dancer kissed; slobbering over each other as if they were two animals in a feeding frenzy. The dancer slid down between the Dragon's legs and began unzipping his pants. *"Zip!"* she whispered. She began slurping with loud satisfaction. The Dragon growled as he ejaculated into her mouth. Their play had ended as quickly as it had started. The limousine drove around the busy streets of China Town, out by the Fisherman's Wharf, and back to Chinatown. The whole time the man growled and the dancer placed her head on his shoulder as if they were a happy couple sight seeing in San Francisco. They were dropped off in a dark alley somewhere in Chinatown. The Dragon, and the partially dressed dancer entered the carnivore's den.

The den was in a rooftop studio with a spectacular view of the San Francisco Bay. Partitions divided the spacious living room into a living area and a dining area. The living area had a corner featuring large statue of Jesús. The scent of fresh and burnt incense filled the air. The center of this area was filled with pillows and small eating tables where eating on the floor is customary. The Dragon guided his prey to the pillows where he grabbed the dancer's clothing, and began to pull away the skirt and leggings. They kept kissing the whole time the Dragon undressed the dancer until she was completely naked from the waist down, revealing the transvestite target that the monster had followed and studied for more than a year. The Dragon's strong arms flipped the dancer on her stomach and began to sodomize her while holding to the dancer's penis in one hand and feeling for a scalpel in his coat's pocket with his other hand. *A sure kill,* he thought. The dancer pushed back and adjusted her buttock for better penetration. The Dragon's eyes rolled around in his head as he reached for the dancer's throat. As he climaxed, his fingers squeezed the life out of the dancer. She tried to pull his fingers away from her throat, but he was too strong and too heavy of a load on her back to fight. Her body collapsed on the floor with the Dragon on her back.

The dancer's body went limp as she coughed, gasping for her last breaths of air. Before losing consciousness, she saw a figure dressed in black attack the Dragon, knocking him off her back. Before blacking out, she saw an arm reach down and felt the back of her head come to rest on a soft pillow.

The police found signs of a struggle. The body of homicide victim, a Chinese businessman landed up against a large statue of Jesús, about ten feet away from where they found the dancer. The autopsy showed that the businessman had died of severe head trauma, clearly inflicted by an intruder who interrupted the assault. The dancer, a well known transvestite performer in a Chinatown club, was found unconscious, but alive, with a severely bruised thorax. His name was withheld from any of the police records and newspaper articles and it was believed that he had been placed under a police relocation program. Behind the Christ statue, the police found altar offerings: 8 pink roses were placed on a red stain cloth, a mostly burnt-down, Chinese funerary structure, two bowls of rice, a surgical knife, and little candles bordering the roses. Six newspaper clippings of a serial killer named, "The Man Killer", were scattered on the floor of the altar, implicating the Dragon to a series of transvestite homicides.

*   *   *   *   *

Captain Williams arranged for Diego and Chi to meet at the SFPD Southern Station on Bryant Street with a forensic technician and an investigator who had written the report on the 8 Roses Case. The report detailed a possible connection with the 10 Roses Case, the 5 Star Hotel homicide case, and a potential lead to the 9 Roses Case. Captain Masoni of the Forensics Division and Lt. Johnson from the Investigation Division welcomed Diego and Chi and walked them over a conference room where the files of the 8 Roses

Case were located. The room was well lit, highlighting the shadows under Diego and Chi's eyes, indicative of fatigue and sleep deprivation.

Capt. Masoni and Lt. Johnson were serious men who protected the reputation of their division and department by sticking to the facts and not conjuring theories of possible suspects; especially in the discussion of unsolved murders.

The SFPD had become notorious for its attitude of shooting first and then asking questions. In recent years, the department had been widely scorned for its practice of justifying excessive force and sloppy forensics, which created a dangerous and symbiotic confusion of reality and fiction. Evidence had the habit of appearing out of thin air, or disappearing as if it never existed. All in all, Capt. Masoni and Lt Johnson knew they had to protect the credibility of SFPD.

Capt. Masoni introduced himself to his colleagues from the Berkeley Police Department, "Captain Masoni! Pleased to meet you Captain Williams."

Capt. Williams shook hands, "pleasure to see you again and these are our detectives Diego de Campos and Chi Ling."

Lt. Johnson stepped forward and extending his hand, "Captain Williams thank you for briefing us about the case so we can prepare ourselves for this meeting."

"Detective Ying!" said Chi with a controlled smile.

After reviewing the files and writing some significant findings on the smart board, Diego asked the two police administrators, *"Are either of you familiar with the funerary art structures in the Man Killer case, or as we call it, the 10 Roses case?"* asked Chi.

"Do you mean the wax structure that was mostly burnt to the base?" asked Lt. Johnson.

"Yes," said Chi. *"The one with multiple wicks on its face."*

Captain Masoni, *"All in all, other than the physical structure itself, we do not have much on it."*

"It may be related to Chinese funerary art?" said Chi rhetorically.

"Lt. Johnson, *ask department staff if anyone knows anything about Chinese funerary art,"* ordered Captain Masoni. Lt. Johnson left immediately to dispatch the announcement.

Diego recreated the crime scene with the evidence found in the files: an altar was decorated with religious offerings including: a red satin cloth, a burnt funerary structure, different sized marbles, candles, pictures of Chinese people dressed in full religious and military clothing, eight pink roses, a surgical knife, an advertisement of the Dickens' Faire, a statue of Jesús and newspaper articles of transvestite homicides.

The Chronicle reported a homicide in Chinatown; the victim, a Chinese man dressed in a business suit had sustained severe trauma to the head. A transvestite was found unconscious from an attempted asphyxiation. The transvestite had DNA from the Chinese businessman under her nails and the businessman had fingernail scratches from the transvestite.

"Is the victim still alive and can we talk with her?" asked Diego with excitement, looking at Chi.

"Yes, she is still alive and in our relocation program," said Lt. Johnson.

Captain Masoni gave Lt. Johnson a stern look as if to say he did not planned on sharing this information with the Berkeley Police Department. He thought that if another police department solved this case, it would look bad for the SFPD and his leadership. On the other hand, in the wake of the Golden Dragon Massacre, a gang related mass murder in the Chinatown District, if we solve the Dragon homicide, the Chinatown community would be elated. "We will arrange an interview with the survivor of the Man Killer homicide, Chinatown's serial killer."

Chi's eyes glowed as if light was illuminating from them. She felt happy for Diego's quest to pop this case wide open. A street officer from the Northern Station entered the room and introduced himself and volunteered to answer questions on the Chinese funerary art.

"Gentlemen, and Officer Ling," said officer Lee.

"Do we know each other? I don't believe we've met?" asked Chi with a puzzled look.

"Read about you on Berkeley PD's website, glad to meet you. You were in Oakland before, right?" answered Lee with a question.

"Yes! What can you tell us about the Man Killer's Case?" asked Chi.

"Not much about the case, but I do know about the Chinese funerary art mentioned in the dispatch." answered Officer Lee.

"Please go on," encouraged Diego. Captain Masoni waved his hands in approval of dissemination of highly sensitive information with BPD.

"There used to be an art gallery at Fisherman's Wharf, near Ghirardelli Square that promoted an artist from Sacramento by the name of Bo Nianzu. He was devoted to creating funerary art," said Lee capturing everyone's attention.

"You said used to be, what happened to the gallery?" asked Captain Masoni, pushing himself forward to stand next to Officer Lee.

"It closed down because the collector died and Nianzu disappeared from the face of this planet. He is probably hiding out in Chinatown or he has gone to live in China," continued Officer Lee.

"How come you have not volunteered this information before?" asked Lt. Johnson.

"No one has ever asked me about Chinese funerary art before!"

74

replied Officer Lee in defense.

Chi sat down next to the computer and began to search the web for funerary art and Chinese art collectors; Bo Nianzu's link came up. Nianzu created and collected Chinese character statues for the ultimate purpose of selling them to wealthy Chinese. Nianzu collected Chinese funerary art ranging from $10,000-30,000 a piece. Nianzu's art creations should be purchased by museums and preserved for future generations to enjoy and admire, nonetheless, influential Chinese people were willing to spend their life's fortune to burn one at their family's funeral.

"Can we locate Nianzu?" asked Chi.

"After the Golden Dragon Massacre, Nianzu went underground. Some people believe he has gone back to China, but I think he is still here in Chinatown," said Officer Lee definitively.

"Why did Nianzu's Chinese funerary art pieces appear at the Claremont Hotel homicide and the Dickens' Faire Homicides?" questioned Diego?

Diego discovered why the Nine Roses Case had slipped through his fingers. Theoretically, the crime scene did not have an altar. The homicide victim was laid out in the middle of the stage and was surrounded with candles, antique dolls dressed in the Dickens' era, nine lavender roses, and a Chinese funerary statue; from Nianzu's collection and a brochure of the Omni Hotel in San Francisco.

Written on whiteboard:

# Homicides	Crime Scene	Public Event	Victim
Six Roses	Gilroy	Garlic Festival	Child Molester
Seven Roses	Santa Cruz	Board Walk	Child Molester
Eight Roses	San Francisco	Chinatown	Mankiller
Nine Roses	San Francisco	Cow Place	Dickens Faire Actor
Ten Roses	Berkeley	Omni/Claremont Hotel	Male Escort

(a dozen red roses found in bedroom with note: Love thy self, Cecilia)

Diego pointed to the white board: *"Gentlemen!"* Diego summarized the evidence and linked them to the different Rose Cases. *"We have five homicides that happened on an average of three years apart and they contain the same evidence: a red satin cloth, a Chinese Candelabra, candles, pictures of people, food, burning incense, roses signifying an order or sequence of their occurrence, newspaper articles implicating the victim, and promotional publications pointed to the next Rose homicide."*

Captain Masoni stepped forward and took control of the rest of the meeting, *"Great work team, we have connected the dots to the workings of a Serial Killer's Killer. Congratulations!"*

"We need to find Nianzu, the funerary art collector!" Chi interrupted. *"We need to know why his artwork keeps appearing at these homicides."*

Diego jumped in and said, *"We need to find out more about this Serial Killer's Killer. We think that he has committed ten homicides and we don't know how many more there will be before we catch him. We need to prevent the next homicide: the Eleven Roses Case. We know that it will happen at one of the next three Gilroy Garlic Festivals, as indicated by the Gilroy Garlic Festival promotional brochure and the 11 garlic heads left at the crime scene of the 10 Roses Case."*

Captain Williams walked in and was briefed, *"Maybe we can*

learn more about this Serial Killer's Killer by working backwards from the 10 Rose Case."

Chapter 9

Broken Men

Father Ignacio

Father Ignacio was raised in an orphanage in Santa Cruz County, California. Down a long dirt road with vineyards on both sides sits a large red brick building with walnut trees circling it. The place is known as St. Jude's, an orphanage full of unwanted children. Most of the children at St. Jude had been abandoned but a few were the secret offspring of nuns living at the nunnery near the Saint Mary's Catholic Church. From time to time, lonely priests came to the nunnery to conduct mass or have a cup of tea, and sometimes the inadvertent result was a pregnancy, kept hidden under a habit, or in some cases, ended by another sister, responding to a cry of desperation. Behind the orphanage was a secret cemetery with three small gravestones that only the nuns and the priests knew about. While these men and women gave their souls to God, they were still housed in a human body, and had human needs, and for that they paid dearly for their sins. In secrecy and in shame, they did their daily penance to gain forgiveness from all who were wounded from their acts.

Ignacio did not grow up knowing his last name; he was called Father Ignacio as long as he could remember. All the children at the orphanage knew that they were there because their parents couldn't care for them. Some suspected that some nuns were their mothers because a particular nun would pay more attention to one child more than she did to other children. A nun would take a child for a long walk down the dirt road, sometimes in the company of a priest. Some children didn't have any visitors and the nuns were too busy to divide up their time equally with the children who didn't have visitors.

Until Father Ignacio was almost ten years old, he had no real friends and he prayed alone. He was very shy and self-conscious; he dragged his feet and had a hard time looking any adult in the eyes. Nonetheless, over the next ten years, he became a favorite of two priests, both of whom he came to revere and trust. In his role as altar boy and confidant, each made him feel special and loved.

He came to understand that he had been called by God to serve the Church and to care for the sacramental needs of its priests. Since he was mainly seen in the company of clergy, the kids and the nuns called him Father Ignacio. When the Archbishop came to visit St. Jude's, he was introduced as "Father Ignacio." The Bishop also took an interest in Ignacio. The Bishop would call St. Jude's and ask for Ignacio. Ignacio had a wonderful smile and copper hair, which made him look like an angel. The Bishop liked to surround himself with angels. Ignacio learned that by giving himself to God, the Archbishop, and the priests, he could forget the first ten years of his life, a time when he felt abandoned and unloved. Now the kingdom of heaven had opened up for him.

At eighteen years of age, Father Ignacio was appointed by the Bishop to serve as his personal aide, a role that Father Ignacio took very seriously. Five years later the Bishop took ill and Ignacio was permanently at his side until he passed away on a cold December morning. Due to the Bishop's last official orders, Ignacio was admitted to a seminary to become a priest. *Imagine*, he thought, *this worthless orphan will become a priest*! Ignacio knew the role of being a priest all too well and decided that he, too, would have an aide to mentor and to love.

In the first years after Ignacio was ordained, he was assigned to different parishes, each for a three-year stay. Upon each new arrival, he immediately searched out a favorite person to befriend. Father Ignacio was young and looked more like a Hollywood actor than a priest. His copper hair still attracted attention, but it was his smile and those black eyes that won everyone's heart. Father Ignacio could easily disarm those who distrusted him. When he was speaking, he had a way of making a person feel that they were the only one in the room. His manner of shaking hands was to take his parishioner's right hand between his hands and squeeze it with a loving smile. Everyone felt he was doing God's work.

Within a month after Father Ignacio arrived for a ten year stay at the Catholic Church at Gilroy, the attendance almost doubled. Father Ignacio did not need to read directly from the scriptures or his notes to deliver the sermon; divine inspiration just seemed to flow out of his mouth. People were drawn to his assurance that God would take care of them, and that Jesús loved each and every one. *"God, loves you, yes, you!"* he would say, and then repeat softly so that everyone would feel as if he was talking to them personally. In less than a year, his sermon was at capacity a half hour before the service started. The other priests were lucky to have twenty to thirty people at attendance of their sermons; nonetheless, they had no resentment towards Father Ignacio's popularity. *"Yes, Jesús loves you, yes, you!"*

Juan Carlos Óbregon

The evolution of the human race has been based on the premise that God has with each creation enhanced his work. Such was the case when Juan Carlos García Óbregon was born. The whole community acknowledged that Juan Carlos was a special child. When he was a baby, everyone made incomprehensible chatter at the child with big honey brown eyes and dark black hair; each time he smiled, everyone smiled back. Even Father Ignacio praised the Óbregon family for the delivery of God's special child. He baptized Juan Carlos joyfully. *"I hope I am still at St Mary's when Juan Carlos has his first communion,"* prayed Father Ignacio. He asked the Óbregon family if Juan Carlos could become an altar boy, but Juan Carlos had little interest in any church activity, including being an altar boy.

All the Óbregons were good-looking people: straight white teeth, big lips, big brown or black eyes, and beautiful hair, but there was no question in everyone's mind that Juan Carlos was "El más guapo," the most handsome of all the boys. Every Mexican family also has an "Endeared One" in the family, usually a girl; in the Óbregon family, Juan Carlos was el más guapo and el Consentido.

Everyone in the family was content to give Juan Carlos the attention that his good looks deserved.

While Juan Carlos athleticism in high school football, wrestling, and track further amplify his popularity. His grades were not stellar; nonetheless, he remained in the top ten percent of class. Yet, while most girls at school liked Juan Carlos, not one of them could claim she was his girlfriend. During his junior year in high school, Juan Carlos joined the Future Teachers of America Club. Most of the members of the club were girls. It was at a Future Teachers of America meeting where he first laid eyes on his dream girl.

Rosa Santos, a transfer student from Hollister, saw Juan Carlos at an FTA club meeting for the very first time. While she had the same reaction as everyone did when they first laid eyes on Juan Carlos, she tried everything possible to not show her attraction to him. She instinctively knew that she could not let Juan Carlos know that she thought he was handsome because he would then treat her like he treated all the other girls. When she exited the door, Rosa pretended she had no interest in meeting him or staying after the meeting to speak with him.

In the hallway, Juan Carlos caught up to Rosa. She was more beautiful up close and tall for a Hispanic girl. *"Rosa, right?"* he asked. *"I'm Juan Carlos!"*

"Yes, Rosa Santos," she replied with restraint and continued walking. Hollister lamented the transfer of Rosa to Gilroy, their archrival in sports and academic performance. Rosa was at the top of her junior class, with the highest test scores in school. *"What do you want, Juan Carlos?"* she asked as if irritated by him walking with her.

"Nothing!" he said nervously while continuing to walk at her fast pace. *"I just wanted to introduce myself,"* he said in defeat and fell back behind her.

Rosa continued walking. When she was five steps ahead of him, she turned and said, *"Well, are you going to give up that easy?"* giving him permission to walk alongside her. From that moment on Juan Carlos did not leave her side at school and after school. If one moment was to be the moment to define their relationship, it was that moment. Juan Carlos followed Rosa's initiative; wherever she went, he was her shadow. She did not degrade him in anyway, but Juan Carlos would do anything that Rosa wanted. Everyone could see that they were two beautiful people in love. They were seen together at school activities, community activities and over time, they started parking at Christmas Hill Park so they could have some privacy."

Juan Carlos graduated from high school without much fanfare. He did not want to go away to college and leave Rosa behind. Because of his popularity he did not have trouble finding jobs when he wanted to work.

Rosa Santos graduated with honors and was invited to attend four of the nation's most prestigious universities: Princeton, Harvard, Norte Dame, and Stanford.

"¿Quién es el más guapo de los Óbregones?" Rosa teased. *"Juan Carlos!"* she cheered.

"Who is the smartest girl in Hollister and Gilroy High Schools?" Juan Carlos asked, knowing full well that Rosa had once again earned the highest test scores in her senior class. One would wonder how Rosa Santos could get such high-test scores when she spent so much time with Juan Carlos. Rosa Santos was better wired to solve problems than most people, but it would be everybody else's problems she would solve, and not her own.

Time can be a fluid phenomenon. Being in love one day can seem to last forever, and at the same time, years can pass in the blink of an eye. That summer, Juan Carlos won the lottery to serve his country in Vietnam. Of course, he passed his physical exam. At the Greyhound station, the Óbregons and Santos families gathered to bid him farewell. Juan Carlos and Rosa kissed each other so hard that their teeth cut their lips. He boarded the bus, not suspecting that his true love and his likeness in her belly were left watching the bus pull out of the station.

Her last words to him floated in the air as the bus roared out of the station, *"¡Qué vayas con Dios, mi amor!"*

By his third mission, Juan Carlos had demonstrated his courage on three different occasions, taking huge risks to carry badly wounded soldiers out of the firefight to safety where they could be seen by a medic. He saved a few lives and was decorated for his bravery. One soldier from Kentucky died while he was carrying him to safety. In his mind, to this day, Juan Carlos is still carrying this dead soldier to safety.

Juan Carlos wrote to Rosa every day, but he did not know if she was getting his letters. Because he was moving camps almost every week, he did not receive any letters from Rosa or his family for months, neither did anyone else in his platoon. War was an ungodly hell: bombs exploding around him every day, smoke clouding the air he breathed. Sleeping under those conditions was nearly impossible. The soldiers and officers did not function at their best because they were sleep-deprived.

A corporal woke Juan Carlos up one morning to give him a letter that announced that he was a father. Doctor Young had assisted Rosa with the delivery of a nine-pound baby boy named after him, Juan Carlos Junior. From that day on, he began thinking that he needed to be more careful while out on patrol. For him, it was as if he now had to do everything possible to get himself home in one piece.

One dark night on patrol, JC, as his buddies called him, heard something a few yards away. He left his foxhole to investigate the noise and stepped on a land mine; the explosion killed two soldiers in his patrol; another besides Juan Carlos was badly injured. Juan Carlos had lost too much blood and the medics had trouble keeping him alive. He and the other soldier were flown out in a helicopter to the nearest military hospital where the doctors operated on Juan Carlos. He was unconscious for weeks, until finally the skin grafts healed and he was able to come out of a heavily-drug induced fog.

Juan Carlos was sent home on a medical discharge. He was the only one in his platoon to return home alive. The other soldier who was badly injured died of an infection. Juan Carlos lost both of his legs and one arm. The army fitted him with two prosthetic legs and an arm. He learned how to use his new arm, but he struggled, walking with his new legs.

After six months in United State Army hospitals, a U.S. Army vehicle delivered Juan Carlos to the front door of Rosa's mother's house.. Rosa came out to see who was honking the horn, she saw Juan Carlos struggling to get his legs out of the car. Rosa wanted to cry, her heart felt stuck in her throat causing her to cough. *"My God, what have they done to my man?"* she thought.

"Now, who is this little bundle you are carrying?" asked Juan Carlos grinning.

"Juan Carlos Junior, my darling," she exclaimed. *"It is so wonderful to see you!"* She took the sleeping bundle and handed it to Juan Carlos. He took his son in his arms and lost his balance, having to lean back against the car door to keep from falling down with the baby. Juan Carlos became very upset that he couldn't even carry his own baby without fearing that he would drop him. He gave the baby back to Rosa and walked up to her and kissed on her face. The commotion woke up the baby and he started crying. Since she was still nursing Junior, she pulled out her left breast and nursed him. He settled down almost instantly.

Over the next three months, with federal assistance for veterans, Juan Carlos was able to open a small cantina in the same block as the Conejeras, labor camp He also purchased a cabin that was attached to the cantina for Rosa and Juan Carlos Junior. Since he could no longer make love to Rosa in the way she was accustomed to, Juan Carlos prepared a living studio out of the storage room in the cantina and there is where he slept. Rosa visited Juan Carlos daily and brought him food and washed his clothes. When Juan Carlos Junior started walking, Juan Carlos forbid her to call him Carlitos Óbregon, so he grew up as Carlos Santos. Carlitos was also forbidden to play in the cantina. Rosa hired a cousin to be with Carlitos while she worked in the Cantina. The door between the Cantina and Rosa's cabin was left open almost every night she and Carlos drank themselves to sleep.

Juan Carlos forbade Rosa to call their son Juan Carlos, *"Rosa," call your son Carlos and not Juan Carlos,"* he begged Rosa while crying silently. *"I am no longer a man, or a lover. I don't want him growing up knowing that his father is a cripple, a broken man."* They closed the cantina, propped the door open between the cabin and the cantina and fell asleep on his bed. *The tension on their faces escaped into their dreams of yesteryear. Their eyes twitched as they entertained the nostalgic days when they first met. In the dreams where there is no time, the realization of their reality caused their eyes to swell and water. They were together in their dreams, living a happier life than the one they had to wake up to. Rosa's naked body rested on Juan Carlos' chest; on the floor, the prosthetic legs and arm were piled on top of their clothes.*

Juan Mercado-El Mero Chingón

Don Juan's backhand landed on little Juanito's face before he could duck or move away. A kick on the butt usually followed. Juanito managed to avoid the boot by moving sideways and running out of the house. Although he was only eight years old, he was always anticipating some kind of abuse from his father. Don Juan was simply a mean son of a bitch. He physically abused his wife for no reason. When asked why he had administered a particular punishment? He would say, "I don't need a reason, you son of a bitch!"

Every time little Johnny was beaten by Don Juan, he promised himself, *"¡Un día lo voy a matar!* One day, I am going to kill him!"

One day, like many days, Don Juan came home drunk and beat up his whole family. The furniture in the room was always in some state of repair. Juanito called out, *"Tornado!"* and everyone ran out of the house. Everyone in the family had secretly thought of killing Don Juan.

At fourteen years of age, Juanito had decided he was not about to get another beating from Don Juan. He ran away from home in order to prevent himself from killing his father. He joined a group of farm workers and immigrated to the United States. Once there, he wanted to buy a car, but he was not old enough to drive. While working in the strawberry fields in Watsonville, he got a part-time job at an auto repair shop. The back of the auto repair shop looked like a cemetery of abandoned cars used for car parts. Juanito was industrious and goal-oriented. He wanted a car, so he started fixing an abandoned 55 Chevy. During his breaks and days off, he worked on the Chevy.

Unbeknownst to Juanito, the 55 Chevy belonged to Billy Goodman, who also worked at the auto repair shop. Goodman lacked the initiative to get his car running again. When he saw Juanito working on his car, he didn't object, until one day, when Juanito started the 55 Chevy. Billy approached him, *"Hey, where are you going with my car?"*

"This 55 Chevy is my car," declared Juanito, waving his arms over the cemetery of cars. *"I put this car together with parts from all those cars. It is mine!"*

Billy stepped in front of the Chevy. The owner of the shop and two other mechanics came out to see what all the yelling was about. *"Hey, what is the problem here?"*

"This mojado is stealing my car. Tell the wetback that the Chevy is my car," he demanded.

"You have not touched the Chevy since you parked it in my cemetery over two years ago and now that it's fixed you say you want it," said the owner. *"Juanito fixed it, so the Chevy belongs to Johnny. He asked me if he could fix a car from all the abandoned cars, and I said 'give it a shot'. Billy, if you want the Chevy give Juanito $200, since he fixed it, and then it's yours again. If not, it belongs to him."*

Billy attacked Juanito. Billy, being five years older and much bigger than Juanito, knocked him over and they rolled around on the ground kicking and punching each other. They separated and stood up glaring at each other with hate in their eyes.

"You son of a bitch!" screamed Billy.

"¡Hijo de la chingada!" screamed Juanito.

The two of them threw themselves at each other like rabid dogs. This was the day Juanito became known as Juan. He was more athletic than Billy. When Billy swung his arm at Juanito's face, Billy was hit repeatedly on the face with rights and lefts. Billy tried kicking him, only to have his leg caught, twisted, and thrown to the ground.

Having had a mean father had prepared Juan for the many confrontations he was going to have with rough people throughout his life. However, it did not prepare him for having a loving family. He did not have a good role model for a father, nor did he have the faintest idea how to be a husband. He learned from his father that the way to raise a family is to beat them to submission. He ruled with fear. Fear was what he learned to live with all his childhood. And as much as he told himself that he knew better, his father's emotional DNA was part of his make-up.

Juan married Rosalinda Calderón and moved to a labor camp in Pajaro, near Watsonville. Rosalinda had one child after another, and it wasn't long before Juan, like his father before him, cursed at his children, *"Son una bola de pendejos, you good for nothing son of bitches."*

Two years after his son, Juan Mercado III, was born, the family was evicted from the labor camp because the police had been called too many times. He packed up his family and all their belongings and drove over Hecker Pass towards Gilroy, California. Before reaching town, the 55 Chevy ran out of gas, throwing Juan into a rage that would tear the family into thousands of fragile pieces of glass. He slugged, kicked, and threw things at everyone in the family, including his pregnant wife.

Yiwu Yungfu Zhou

The Cross-Continental Railroad connected the Atlantic Ocean to the Pacific Ocean, propelling the United States of America into a global economic presence for centuries to come. These times generated a type of idealism and a mindset that there was no venture that could not be realized in America. Cargo ships with merchandise from all over the world hovered at sea ports like migrating butterflies around an entire tree, thrusting America into the future without the ability to look at itself. America did not look back because it was too busy dealing with the future: the telephone, airplanes all at breakneck speed.

Like a lot of other cities, the Chinatown in Sacramento grew around the railroad terminal. The Chinese settled down and became contributing members of their community. Chinese populations were fractured by massive deportations over the years; their broken lineages were viewed as loose railroad ties. Many families did not have grandfathers and fathers to guide them through life. For this reason, funerary rituals became important to them. Many Chinese people would say that they had ancestors back to the Zhou Dynasty. The Chinese from Sacramento's Chinatown were proud to say that anything that can be found in

China could be found in Sacramento: these included exotic commodities, oddities like grown bear claws and medicinal plants, everything that is, except their fathers and grandfathers.

In Gilroy, only a few Chinese lived among the Whites and Mexicans: they were called "Chinamen" by the Whites and "Chinitos" by the Mexicans, When one particular "Chinaman" moved from Gilroy to Hood, along the Sacramento River, just south of Elk Grove, he brought all his belongings in a knapsack and lived among the Chinese people in Hood's Chinatown. He introduced himself as Yiwu Yungfu. He found refuge living in a Chinese community knowing that he once belonged to someone's heart. The Chinese acknowledged that Yiwu Yungfu was working out some things within himself, redefining something in his inner self. He dressed in dark gray clothing and walked slowly home, carrying his heart in his extended hands. Someone or something had broken his heart. He was beginning to wear his broken heart on his face; deep lines grew outward from his eyes and down his face.

In his shack, he knelt in prayer, surrounded by four walls, whose wooden boards permitted the outside to come in and dance with the flames of the carefully placed candles on the altar. His broken ancestral lineage tormented him; he could not name his ancestors in prayer. His world felt empty not knowing his grandfathers and father, but nothing could compare with the emptiness he felt for his only love. He thought, *Well, at least I experienced what it feels like to love someone and have someone love me, too. I should feel like the happiest person who's ever lived, she loved me more than I loved myself. Then why do I have to live without her?"* he asked himself in silence.

After prayer he practiced martial arts while dressed in a warrior outfit. This Chinese ritual was very important to him. This exercise was the only thing that kept him from thinking about this lost love. When he first came to the Hood community, he often felt that he must throw caution to the wind and go to her the next morning, but when the sun came in through the kitchen window, he knew that he could not go to her, not ever.

Chapter 10

Garlic,

The Stinking Rose

The common garlic is sometimes called "the stinking rose" because when eaten, a pungent odor emanates from the mouth. The stinking rose has been effective as a repellent of birds, mosquitos, rabbits, and moles. For more than five thousand years, garlic has been a popular folk remedy to repel evil forces. In some cultures, people wear garlic wreaths around their necks, hang garlic on doors and rub it into keyholes for protection—specifically, to ward off vampires, werewolves, and demons.

Gilroy, California has the unique distinction of being named the "Garlic Capitol of the World." This status is celebrated annually with the Gilroy Garlic Festival. Organizers play upon the folklore and the medicinal properties of garlic to promote the festival, which celebrates all things made with garlic.

*   *   *   *   *

After two hours of deliberation over the Serial Killer's Killer investigation, the team reached consensus; the evidence indicated that he would strike again within the next three years at the Gilroy Garlic Festivals. Since the 6th Rose case, this serial killer has left evidence announcing the location of the next killing. For the 6 Roses case, it was an advertisement of the Santa Cruz Boardwalk, for the 7 Roses case, it was a brochure of the Dickens' Faire, and now in the 10 Roses case, the killer left eleven garlic heads and a brochure about the Garlic Festival. The important question to answer is: when will he strike again? Captain Williams, Diego, Chi, and four other detectives and a stenographer sat around a table with their heads on overdrive. The Gilroy Police Department, with the help of the FBI, decided to start the surveillance of the next festival with four times the number of security than before. Law enforcement was under heavy pressure to solve the Rose Cases before he struck again; although the public was beginning to see him as another crime fighter, someone above the law carrying out justice more efficient than law enforcement.

94

Somehow, information about the Rose Cases was leaking to the news media and the FBI was furious about it. Consequently, fewer people were invited to high-level discussions on the Rose Cases. In obvious desperation, Captain Williams attempted to arrange for Chi and Diego to interview a witness under relocation protection by the San Francisco Police Department. In the meantime, Diego and Chi were dispatched to hit the streets of San Francisco's Chinatown and to inquire about the whereabouts of Bo Nianzu, the artist whose funerary art sculptures were found at each of the Rose crime scenes.

At a crosswalk, Chi pulled on Diego's shoulder in a caring way, not allowing him to cross the intersection on a yellow light. *"Look around you,"* Chi whispered without moving her lips. *"We are being watched."*

Diego stepped back up onto the curb, put his arms around Chi and pretended to kiss her on the neck; thanking her for not letting him walk right into the traffic.

"No! Not!" Chi protested pushing him away.

"You started it!" Diego fired back.

"I thought you were not interested in relationships, anyway?" asked Chi stepping back.

"Look, we are being watched, let's pretend we are a couple in love."

"Ok," Chi grabbed his shirt and walked closer to Diego.

"I counted four people following us," added Diego.

"Did you see the elderly Chinese woman standing by the street post? She's watching us too. She'll walk a bit, stop, turn around and look for us, and then continues walking," Chi added.

Diego stopped at the streetlight and pretended to want to kiss Chi while he looked around her back for unusual suspects. She weakly pushed him away. *"I am just...!"* muttered Chi.

"Sorry, me too," mumbled Diego.

They started laughing and continued to walk without worrying about who was watching them or who was following them. They walked through the alley where the 8th Rose Case had taken place. *"Here is where the dancer was attacked,"* pointed Diego.

The dancer asked for protection because she feared the Dragon 's limo driver knew she had survived the attack. According to the word out in the community, the same limo driver had driven the Dragon to all his killings. The dancer was frightened, knowing that someone out there thought that she was somehow responsible for the death of the Dragon, who had come to be known by the police as the Mankiller. The driver had a good look at the dancer but the dancer was not able to see the driver's face. The files mentioned that she thought that he might have been Chinese, but she could not swear to it; he was wearing a black driver's cap shielding most of his face so she saw only the side of his head.

Diego's mobile phone buzzed in his coat pocket. The San Francisco Police Department was prepared to arrange an interview with the dancer. *"Yes, this is detective de Campos,"* answered Diego.

"Where are you?" asked the dispatcher.

"We are at the corner of Broadway and Stockton Street, near the New Moon restaurant," answered Diego

"Wait there and an unmarked black car will pick you up in fifteen." directed the dispatcher.

"Copy that!" replied Diego.

"SFPD is coming for us," Diego directed his attention to Chi.

Diego hoped that SFPD would take their time, *"Should we hide from them?"*

"Oh shut up!" Chi punched him in the belly softly.

There were only two people watching them by the time an unmarked car drove up to the curb and interrupted their chase.

"Are you two an item….?" asked the driver.

"We were being followed," answered Chi defensively.

"Can't say I didn't like it," added Diego.

"Oh shut up, Diego," elbowed Chi laughing.

The driver pulled into an alley where another unmarked car was waiting. Diego and Chi stepped out of one unmarked police car and into another one. When the two cars came out of the alley and they turned in opposite directions. A few fast turns, in and out of several alleys and suddenly the car drove into a garage and stopped and the garage door closed behind them. Diego and Chi were led into a dark apartment, and from there, into a bedroom with a small lamp that shed light on a figure that was in prayer, facing a life size Buddha statue. A young Chinese female dressed in traditional clothing stood up and turned to face Diego and Chi.

The Dancer extended her arm, inviting Chi and Diego to sitting area on the floor. Her face was painted with the traditional Geisha white makeup. She looked absolutely beautiful. Each move was choreographed: her head tilting slowly and turning sideways as if by remote control. The Dancer was always performing. She was obviously accustomed to playing the role of a dancer who also provided sexual pleasures. There is no shortage of clients who will pay top dollar to be entertained and indulge in the desires of the flesh, some of them need to experience the sense of superiority and power that they get when they are able to dominate another man.

"What do you want to know?" she asked as if to start a song.

"You are the only witness that we know who has seen the Rose Killer. You saw his face, right?" asked Diego appearing somewhat desperate.

"Well, Yes! I saw his black face, but it was difficult to distinguish his facial features because he was wearing black clothing." the Dancer stood up and paced to the door and back. *"He had his head covered with a black hood, or something black because his whole body seemed black, from head to foot."* The Dancer's face began to glisten as she spoke. The perspiration began to ruin her make-up. The mascara ran down her face, painting black tears on her painted white cheeks. *"I surmise that the mystery killer killed the businessman, and then placed my head on the pillow, I saw into his eyes, he had black contact lenses, the ones that covered the white of eyes too, all black, the whole eyeball. I know because I too wear colored contact lenses when I dance, but not ones like those."* The elegant dancer took out a mirror and with a white scarf wiped the cheeks clean and with much care she re-applied the make-up.

"Is it possible that he painted his face black, rather than being a Black person?" questioned Diego.

"Yes, it's possible!" answered the dancer with a frozen smile. She could still see his kind face.

"I read your interview and you also said, "I think he was Asian" but that you couldn't swear on it?" questioned Chi.

"Yes, his eyes were almond-shaped," she said in desperation. *"I felt kindness in those eyes."* In her business she had learned to read the eyes, whether a client was violent or kind. Most of them were broken men who let out their pain on someone less fortunate than them.

"Ok, if he is Asian, then most likely, he is not Black, which means that he painted his face black to camouflage his identity," concluded Chi.

"I think he is Asian, look at the funeral offerings; a red stain cloth and funerary art from Nianzu's collection was found at all the crime scenes," argued Diego.

"You are not looking at the important facts," the Dancer insisted

on another focus. *"There have been hundreds of transvestites killed in the last ten years and the police have not found one of their killers. Society sees us at the bottom of the heap of humanity and the police department does not care about us. This vigilante killer does care about us. He is protecting us."*

"You are right!" jumped in Chi. *"There are too many transvestites being killed,"* cried Chi. *"You are right! Help us!"*

"To begin with, the Man Killer is not the only one killing us!" The Dancer pointed her finger at Chi, *"Do the research; we have many different predators roaming the streets in the Bay Area, soliciting sex from transvestites and killing us. You catch'em, and you let them go because you supposedly do not have enough credible evidence to arrest them. Crimes against transvestites are not viewed important. It happens again and again,"* she snapped, with obvious disdain. *"Somebody is finding these killers and is doing your job,"* she turned her head away and started to walk out of the room, stopped, turned around and said, *"Maybe you should spend your energy on helping the Rose Case Killer capture more killers! Perhaps this serial killer's killer cares more about us than law enforcement."* She danced out of the room and the curtains hanging from the doorway closed behind her.

Two men appeared at the door and hurriedly escorted Diego and Chi into the unmarked car. The garage door opened and they were directly driven to Diego's vehicle. At his car, Diego opened the door for Chi, but she did not say anything. She stepped into the seat and settled into it before Diego closed the door.

Once in the police car, Diego was about to start the car, and instead decided to say something to Chi. He looked at her beautiful eyes and sweet smiling face. Before he could utter the first word, Chi reached out her hand and placed it over his mouth. The words did not come out of his mouth, but somehow his feelings and thoughts did. Chi smiled at him, relieving some of the tension in his body.

His cellular phone buzzed, *"Hello, this is Detective de Campos."*

"Diego, this is Carlos, Carlitos. I don't have time to explain, so just listen."

"Carlos! Man! Where have you been?" Diego interrupted.

"Please, we'll talk another time. Just listen," demanded Carlos.

"The FBI is asking questions about you. Internal Affairs has been busy here at Forensics Division asking everyone questions about the Rose Cases. They want to know if we have lab work on you, DNA, finger prints, and your history: family, friends, education, and employment."

"Shit, this is really serious. Why are they looking at me?" asked Diego.

"They are looking at everyone dealing with the Rose cases, but they have an even closer eye on you. They have a suspicion that your success at solving cases is due to you having a link with crime in the Bay Area," Carlos said, *"Talk with you in a week."*

"One-time killers are much easier to apprehend because they usually leave evidence to connect them to their crimes. Serial Killers are intelligent and much older. I have been lucky that I have been smarter than the one-time killers. Serial killers are another matter altogether! What do you mean a week?" asked Diego.

"They are watching me too. Goodbye! Can't be too careful." Carlos abruptly ended the conversation.

"That was a childhood friend of mine who works for Oakland PD Forensics, he says the FBI is watching me. They are the ones following us, well, I guess I mean me." Diego explained.

At the Berkeley Police station, Diego and Chi witnessed Captain Williams yelling at two men in his office. The yelling continued even after they noticed that Diego and Chi entered the office. Diego thought he was going to be grounded to a desk assignment, but instead he was informed that Bo Nianzu, the funerary art artist had been located and that he too is a "person of interest" in this Serial Killer's Killer case.

"Diego, you and Chi are not...?" he didn't finish the question.

"We decided that since we were being followed, we'd pretend we were an ordinary couple enjoying San Francisco," answered Diego confidently and Chi concurred with a nod of her head.

"I thought so!" he exclaimed. *"Those FBI men are giving me ulcers!"* said the Captain and he went back into his office to continue yelling at the FBI. *"He is my best detective!"* The FBI was certain that the SKK is an insider and coincidently, Diego is from Gilroy, the probable target location of the next Rose Case.

*   *   *   *   *

In a black Hearse with tinted windows Chi, Diego, and Captain Williams were chauffeured to an unknown underground facility beneath Chinatown. Chi looked at Diego with astonishment and at the same time felt honored to be in such a high security facility. A fully staffed forensics department worked busily on their research in full view of all who passed by the hallway. In an office with a long table and chairs, two large men in tuxes waited. They turned to face Chi, Diego, and Captain Williams. One of them was clearly the bodyguard: dressed in an all-black tuxedo; and the other wore a tuxedo with a white shirt and ruffled sleeves.

"I am Bo Nianzu, the Chinese funerary art collector whose sculptures were found in the Rose Cases," said Bo bluntly. He was known not to waste time on formalities, life was too short to be Chinese, he'd say. He was a large man, with broad shoulders outlining his block-shaped body. He was in his early fifties with no apparent signs of graying, unless of course, he dyed his hair. He sported thick reading glasses with thick black rims.

"Why are you hiding from the public, Mr. Nianzu?" asked Diego.

"I am not hiding. I am staying away to protect the public. I am

saddened that my spiritual funerary art is part of these horrific rituals," answered Nianzu in defense of his art collection. *"Many years ago, a client of mine received a commission to find a funerary urn for someone who wanted to remain anonymous. He refused to accept the work because it was an art piece with a pre-existing design and he did not accept commission work."*

"Did you ever find out who commissioned the work?" asked Captain Williams.

"No, however my life has been threatened twice and I am not going to give them another chance."

Captain Williams interjected: *" Mr. Nianzu, I have no manners. This is detective de Campos, and Chi,"* somewhat embarrassed for not remembering Chi's last name. He continued, *"and I am Capt. Williams."*

"I know about detective de Campos, Diego, right?" asked Nianzu. "Read about your work in the newspapers."

"Yeah, well I really like your collection of Chinese funerary art and the respect it shows for those that have passed," said Diego.

"Thank you." said Nianzu.

Chi, waiting for an entry, noticed that people were holding their breath and readying to speak next, blustered into the conversation, *"Why do you think that your funerary art is showing up in these Rose Cases?"* Her eyes didn't blink, nor did she take a breath herself until Nianzu spoke his first word.

"Dzidzat!" said Nianzu.

"Chi took a deep breath and exhaled slowly as she said, *"Dzidzat, the Chinese ritual of burning of paper at funerals."* answered Chi.

"If he is not Chinese, this serial killer knows the way of Tao. The Chinese burn paper with writing about the one whose passed, burn his

belongings and what he or she had of value, like money and birth certificates." added Nianzu. *"Dzidzat, is a formal ritual way of protecting them in their journey through the underworld and staying connected so they can be oriented back to their home. It is an alchemy of mortal recipes for an immortal soul."* Nianzu bowed.

"Ok," interrupted Capt. Williams, *"Someone is using your art to give the victims a send-off. Is this what you're saying? Send him off on a journey through the bowels of hell and help him return home?"* Capt. Williams was frustrated, he thought they were not getting anywhere with Nianzu.

"Do you think that the Serial Killer's Killer is Chinese?" asked Chi.

"Yes!" Nianzu quickly replied.

"Why?" asked Diego.

"Because he knows of Dzidzat!" insisted Nianzu. *"And he is a wealthy man. I sell my artifacts in the United States for $30,000 to $50,000. They are even more expensive in the black market. You have to be rich to afford any piece in my collection,"* said Nianzu as he lit a cigarette.

"A rich Chinese who loves funerary art. Hmmm!" speculated Diego.

"How many funerary art pieces have you created? And do you have an inventory of them?" asked Chi.

"Yes, I have owned thirty of them. Ten have been purchased in the United States and two in China. I have three completed ones in my studio, altogether, I have personally created 17 pieces. I don't know how many of them are out in circulation and how many of them have made their way into the black market," said Nianzu.

"We have ten Rose Cases, but not all have Nianzu's funerary art pieces. Who knows how many are in the hands of the serial killer?" concluded Captain with undetermined certainty.

"I know of five that are in private collections and three in museums," added Nianzu.

Nianzu and his bodyguard readied to go out the glass door marked EXIT. Nianzu was not only known for his art collection, Chinese intellectuals considered him to be a spiritual man. Nianzu pledged to assist the FBI to identify the location of his funerary art pieces in circulation, nonetheless, his cooperation did not diminish the suspicion that Nianzu could be the Serial Killer's Killer, "SKK" or had a strong connection with him. The bodyguard opened the door and stepped out first, Nianzu bowed, followed them out, and one of the guards closed the door behind him.

Nianzu's visit had cemented the idea that the serial killer's killer was a rich Asian who practiced the Chinese ritual of altar offerings as a form of ancestral veneration. Dzidzat, "the burning of paper," the idea of attempting to preserve a moment in a world that is so transitory, fascinated the three police officers.

*   *   *   *   *

The roads, highways, and freeways leading to Gilroy during the Garlic Festival in the simmering month of July, get jammed with traffic; they are filled with happy motorists anxious to get into the festival grounds. They come from as far as Canada, through Washington and Oregon down Highway 101 over Pacheco Pass and to Tenth Street, but if they're coming from the coast, the drive goes over Hecker Pass and onto Miller Avenue, the road that leads to Christmas Hill, the home of the festival. As the slow-moving traffic edges closer, the sun seems hotter than usual. Attendees seem to experience a collective amnesia, which enables them, just one year later, to completely forget that it is hot as hell at the Gilroy Garlic Festival. Cars finally arrive at the dirt pit parking lot. With the help of 4,000 volunteers, the three-day festival accommodates upwards of 150,000 people. The people come ready to eat ten tons of beef, four tons of pasta, and two whole tons of garlic. The FREE GARLIC ICE CREAM booth invariably has the longest lines, certainly proving that the ice cream was tasty and different. People wait in line for long periods of time to get drinks and food, to squeeze into the crowded entertainment venues and to pig-out at Gourmet Alley: where the menu features garlic-flavored chicken, beef, 'gator, and buffalo. Most people overeat and being in the blistering temperatures will get some people dizzy; they are fortunate to stagger into a misting tent to cool off. The continuous music is another lifesaver for most people who can't take standing in line in the heat. Even when people may feel they can't eat one more bite, if they haven't had their taste of Garlic French Fries, they force-feed themselves a handful of fries as they walk to their cars. Nobody leaves the Garlic Festival without eating Garlic French Fries.

By 10 am, the traffic for the garlic festival was starting to back up just south of San José on Highway 101 and detective Campos was on duty to hang out at the Gilroy Garlic Festival. The captain gave him two tickets to the festival and required him to have fun at the expense of the FBI. Captain Williams smiled at Diego, knowing very well that he would take Chi to the festival. Chi had been taken off the assignment as Diego's partner and assigned to work with another detective in the Oakland Police Department. Chi was off-duty, but it would never hurt to have another officer on the grounds of the Garlic Festival. Her superior said, *"Have fun, Detective Chi."* Chi was admired because her personality was attractive and she was friendly with everyone.

Diego drove right up to the gate and was allowed entrance into a private parking lot for emergency vehicles and security. A security guard came up to Diego and Chi and asked them to follow him. *"The president of the festival wants to speak with you as soon as you arrive. Keep your entrance tickets handy, you may get lucky and win some prizes."*

Diego and Chi followed through the back of some big tents and into a misting tent. Diego and Chi were sweating, but the misters felt refreshing. *"Mr. de Campos and Miss Ling, welcome to the largest garlic festival in the world,"* the president extended his hand and gave them a huge smile. *"Please let us know if we can be of further help to you. On behalf of the Garlic Festival committee, I want to thank both of you for helping us out with the surveillance."*

"I am not on duty! Just keeping this handsome detective company." declared Chi.

The Gilroy Police Department and the FBI had come to an agreement not to inform the community of the speculation that a Serial Killer's Killer announced that the festival would be the scene of his next homicide. If the public knew about SKK's target, it would dramatically influence the number of people that would attend the festival. Besides, no one could accurately predict at which one of the upcoming festivals SKK would strike. Twenty undercover FBI agents had been assigned to the festival and they were scattered throughout the grounds. Chi had spotted two of the undercover agents field-testing the security by climbing over the fence at the least populated area of the festival. They got in and immediately blended into crowd.

Diego and Chi easily spotted the police and undercover FBI agents. Chi could pick them out in a crowd. It was their behavior that gave them away: pretending not to be on the lookout was a dead giveaway. Diego did not seem too worried about the SKK during their peak hours of the festival. SKK was too clever to work in a public place during their peak hours. He would probably work at night, after the festival was closed, he thought. *"Let's have some fun,"* Diego pulled Chi into the mister and kissed her.

"Let's go to the Wine Pavilion," suggested Chi.

"Ok, but I can only have one glass!" stressed Diego.

"Oh, come on, we are here to enjoy the best gourmet food in the world," Chi teased.

Chi grabbed Diego's hand and pulled him towards the Wine

Pavilion. Suddenly, Diego stopped walking. Chi continued to pull on Diego's arm. Diego appeared to have seen a ghost. He looked carefully at the man pouring wine at the Wine Pavilion. He was pouring himself wine from a bottle he had just opened; he swished the wine around in a deep glass, adored the wine making silky lazy legs on the glass and watching them swim down, and then and only then did he take a slow taste of a Marconi cabernet. Diego decided that this man looked very much like the tennis player in the photos of the Claremont Hotel homicide files. If this is the same man, he had been a friend of the victim, Dr. Cecilia Rollins. Diego and Chi walked up to taste some wine. They listened to a conversation he was having with two friends from Berkeley. Evidently, Stanley traveled and played lots of tennis, primarily at the Claremont Hotel, Club, and Spa. So most likely, it was the same man, Diego thought.

"So, Stanley, why did you get degrees in Religious Studies and History?" the friends asked, teasing him.

"To tell you the truth, I wanted to learn about why religions from around the world seem to promote war on each other. I have always had a fascination for world religions and wanted to understand deeper questions of morality from a good vs evil perspective."

"Well, what kind of job can you get with those degrees, teach at Berkeley?"

"Hey, I just enjoy cultures and languages, languages being my minor; might as well study what you like in life. Don't you think so?"

"Yeah, but what kind of job can you get with those degrees?" they persisted.

"I can get any job I want, if I want a job, I can get it! I am an educated man," he answered with a little agitation.

"I am sorry to interrupt, but I overheard you say that you attended Berkeley," asked Diego.

"Yes, I loved Berkeley! Those years were among the best years of my

107

life!"

"*Me, too!*" answered Diego, taking away some of the discomfort from the other conversation, "*Hi! I am Diego de Campos and this is Chi Ling.*"

"*Hi!*" Chi joined the conversation. "And what is your name?" she asked with a warm smile and taking notes: six foot tall, 200lbs, blond hair, and eyes are blue.

Stanley looked surprised, "*Wait a minute! Did you say Diego de Campos? Are you the same Cal Bear that dominated the wrestling mats?*"

"*The same!*"

"*Wow! Diego de Campos, Berkeley's badass Cal Bear! Hey! I did join the tennis professional circuit for a couple of years. But those tennis players were too fast and strong for me. What are you up to now?*" Stanley paused, and then said, "*How rude of me, not to introduce myself, my name is Stanley Marconi. I volunteer for the Wine Pavilion every year, I represent my uncle's winery which donates much of the wine for the festival,*" Stanley extended his hand and gave them a welcoming smile. Stanley's other friends noted that he was engaged with other customers and left.

"Where did you say you are from, Stanley?" asked Diego.

"Well, I have a hard time with that one. I guess the best answer is the Bay Area. My parents moved a lot, I spent many summers with my grandparents, and I attended mostly boarding schools and private schools growing up," answered Stanley, with hint sadness in his voice.

"I don't have a place that I can really call home either, we were migrant workers—moved around a lot as a child. I call Gilroy my home because I graduated from Gilroy High," Diego attempting at softening the pain.

"*Would you like some wine?*" asked Stanley.

"I would!" answered Chi, not knowing what Diego was thinking. His eyes rolled up to the left.

"Sure, just one taste of Cabernet," answered Diego without taking his eyes from Stanley. He remembered that Marconi had mentioned during the police interview that he was upset that Dr. Rollins' new friends were male escorts. Diego wondered what kind of relationship the tennis pro had had with Dr. Rollins. Stanley continued to pour Chi another glass with a lot more wine than the first time. Diego noticed the extra pour. Chi laughed and pulled Diego aside so that Stanley could not hear their conversation. *"What is going on with you and Stanley?"*

"I recognized his picture from those interviewed at the Claremont Hotel homicide," answered Diego.

Stanley continued to pour wine to other customers and did not seem to be concerned with Chi and Diego watching him from a distance. Chi looked over at Stanley and did not detect any negative feelings from him.

"Don't you think that it is a coincidence that Stanley is here at the next SKK's crime scene?"

"Stay here, I'll be back, I am going to check off my checklist," Chi told Diego as she walked back to get some more wine. *"Stanley, do you work for your uncles' winery?"* asked Chi.

"Well, I wouldn't call it work, detective. They do not actually pay me a salary; since the death of my parents who were killed in an automobile accident, I get a monthly allowance from my inheritance. Besides, I love attending these events sponsored by the Marconi Brothers Wineries, they donate wine and I like the social aspect of serving wine, meeting new people and the small talk," volunteered Stanley as he sipped a bit more wine. *"He added. "I have a soft spot for Gilroy. I grew up here, and first fell in love with a beautiful Mexican girl,"* He swallowed the lump in his throat and continued," *Plus, I love coming to the festival. I met someone this morning who attended Sacred Heart High School in San Francisco at the same time I did."*

"Which events are your favorite places to pour your uncles' wine?" asked Chi to see if he would mention the Claremont Hotel.

Diego had walked back to join Stanley and Chi as Stanley started ticking off the public events that Marconi Brothers sponsored and participated in: *"Santa Cruz Wine Festival, Claremont Hotel Wine Festival, and …."*

"Stanley, what do you recommend we check out while we are here?" asked Diego politely.

"Make time for Gourmet Alley, lots of great food for you to taste!" advised Stanley.

The sun was at high noon and already the heat was stifling. The lines to all the food stands were long. Music could be heard coming from three different places. The crowd was thick and difficult to walk in without bumping into people. Finally they ended up under the misters. Chi hugged Diego and thanked him for bringing her.

"What did you think of Stanley?" asked Diego.

"I did not get any feeling one way or another. I did not sense that he is harboring any kind of resentment or is disillusioned with life." Changing the subject, she brought to his attention that most of the members of the Garlic Festival board were managing the popular events. *"Look at the checklist, they are all working the booths, too."* Chi had checked off most of the names and pictures on the Who's Who of the Garlic Festival. Everyone in town had invested in the Garlic Festival. The festival generates revenue for the local merchants and charitable organizations get large donations from the money generated by the Festival.

"He did seem friendly and open about the information he shared, we'll leave it there for the meantime. We've got homework," answered Diego and moved on to another topic of conversation. Diego's shirt was completely wet and plastered to his body. Chi's hair was dripping wet, as well. The sweat ran in rivulets down her face and

dripped onto her blouse. They were no longer having fun. They walked over to the shade of some trees and listened to the music for a while. Chi's head moved with the country music. She was totally amazing; she liked all types of music including reggae and Cajun.

"Want a beer?" I'll go down there and get us a cold drink," Chi declared sweetly. She walked down from the tree area into the blisteringly sunny area. The Brown Capri pants that she wore mesmerized his vision as she swayed her hips as she walked.

"Please don't turn around," requested a voice from behind Diego. Someone had walked up yo him and was now standing behind a tree. His voice was guttural and he talked slowly. *"Diego, it's Carlos. Don't turn around,"* he said cautiously.

"I have been waiting to hear from you!" exclaimed Diego without turning around. He straightened his body and prepared himself to listen.

"The FBI thinks that you are SKK. To them, everything fits: you're from Gilroy, you have access to police files and you are knowledgeable of forensics," whispered Carlos.

Diego smelled baby powder and heard a baby whimper. *"Carlos, do you have a baby with you?"* asked Diego.

"Yes. Do not turn around. The FBI probably thinks I, too, may be SKK." whispered Carlos.

"Great. So when can we get together?" asked Diego.

"Once the 11ᵗʰ Rose Case is over." Carlos swallowed and choked on his words, *"I don't want the FBI to come poking around my life. I don't want them to think we are working together."*

"I don't have anything to worry about," responded Diego.

"Well, I do! I have a history. I don't want anyone poking into my life's history." Carlos loved his mother; Rosa and he did not want the FBI snooping into their private lives. After Cal Berkeley, he

transferred to San José State University; to be closer to his mother and in five years he completed his education and training in forensic science. He now works in Forensic Analysis Lab for Oakland Police Department, California.

Diego was halfway through his argument, insisting that they meet soon when he noticed that Carlos had disappeared. He turned around and saw a man carrying a front pack with a baby in it disappear into the crowd. In a blink of an eye, Carlos was gone, indistinguishable from anyone else in the stampede of people. Chi emerged out the swarm carrying beer in a paper cup and a cold Gatorade.

They carried their drinks and walked over to Gourmet Alley Food. It was full of people eating under large tents. The food was excellent, gourmet cooking with lots of garlic. As small as Chi was, she could really eat. Diego devoured his plate of assorted meats and garlic fries. Under the tent, the people were too busy eating to talk. Chi stood up and excused herself for a bathroom run. Most of the people had their heads bent down over their plates except for two men with baseball caps looking right at Diego. When Diego looked directly at them, they turned away as if they had not been staring.

"FBI, how obvious!" thought Diego.

Chi returned and without sitting down, she picked up the plates and napkins and said playfully, *"Onward, Christian soldiers!"*

Diego followed suit and stood up, grabbed the plates from Chi's hand and dumped them into a trash bin near the table. At 2 pm, the sun was the hottest of the day. Chi dragged Diego through the rows and rows of booths with arts and crafts and promotional trinkets. Chi had her checklist and was making notes on the pad. *"I have a feeling that many of the people here are related to the victim in the Six Rose Case, the suspected pedophile,"* warned Chi.

"The Garlic Festival is managed by the wealthy farmers.." said Diego sarcastically. *"Well, maybe SKK is one of them, turning his rage*

on his own people." While Diego did make the remark off the cuff, it did make sense. It was no different than the FBI thinking that SKK was a police officer, or former police officer.

While Diego was deep in thought, Chi purchased two Garlic Capitol of the World tee shirts, and handed Diego his. Chi asked, *"Wait for me here, and don't move."* She returned, looking more comfortable in a slim-fitted tee shirt. They stopped at each of the booths and chatted with the people. Chi did not have a problem coming up with things to talk about with the merchants, whereas Diego didn't say much, unless he had a question to ask.

By 5 pm, the crowd had thinned down enough that it was possible to walk around without bumping into people. The events of Day 1 repeated themselves, more or less, for two more days without any difference except for the rotating roster of musicians and their music. After three straight days of beer, Garlic Fries, Garlic Ice Cream, garlic-flavored food, and continuous music; one could become repulsed by the smell of garlic.

The FBI was not happy that SKK was still at large. They gave up the notion that Diego might be SKK. They disappeared from the Gilroy Police Department and promised to be back next year for the festival. The Berkeley Police Department also shifted their resources to the apprehension of other criminals, meanwhile garden-variety killings and stabbings continued unabated throughout the Bay Area. The San Francisco Police Department found the bodies of three transvestites in the trunk of a police car. Killers were making fun of police departments' failed attempts at solving crimes, all crimes. In many cases, police departments knew these suspects were guilty of the crimes, but without more than circumstantial evidence and the testimony of questionable witnesses, their hands were tied. Since he had no responsibility to prove the charges in a court of law, SKK had all the evidence he needed to act swiftly and decisively.

At first, everyone was suspected as being SSK. With Garlic Festival behind them, the police combed through the evidence from the known Roses cases. The victim of the 6 Roses Case came from this community of the well-to-do garlic farmers, a brotherhood akin to a secret society. The other victims were not prominent people in society. SKK did not favor one class over another; apparently, his victims came from all walks of life.

One rainy morning, Diego's cell phone buzzed very early, before sunrise, *"Hello, who's calling this goddam early?"*

He asked in a low voice, *"It's Carlos, Diego! Can we meet today?,"*

"Yes, but why in the name of God are you calling so early?" demanded Diego. Chi, who by now had moved in with Diego, stirred and turned over.

"I am outside your gate," said Carlos. That was no surprise. After all, he, too, was skilled in tracking and finding people. Finding Diego's telephone number was not difficult. Carlos had contacts in most police departments; although he had not met most of them, they were the same crime fighting team.

Diego couldn't get upset because he had wanted to see his old friend, Carlos. He threw off the blankets; his naked body emerging out of the bed. He walked towards a chair where his clothes were draped over its back. He called the guard at the front gate and asked him to direct Carlos to his cottage. He rummaged through the clothes and found his pants, put them on and walked downstairs to the front door. Looking backwards as if someone was following him, Carlos walked slowly to the door. The two old friends embraced; while Diego was still hugging Carlos, Carlos broke away and entered the house.

"How are you doing, Carlos?" asked Diego pushing him back to get a better look at him. "You've become a *Big Man, Vato!"* exclaimed Diego.

"What's with this Hoppers' behavior--why all this secrecy?" asked Diego with annoyance.

"To make a long story short, I am hiding an undocumented immigrant in my house. To complicate things, she's beautiful, I love her and we have a baby. I have no idea how I got myself in this mess." said Carlos, excited to share the news with his best friend.

Diego drew in a deep breath, "Carlitos mi amigo, you got yourself into a real Chingadera, a messy situation. But at the same time, I have to say congratulations—that's one lucky chica." Diego hugged him again.

"Thanks, but it's more complicated than that. Julio Cortez Espinoza, known as El Coyote, a man from Juárez México, is heavily involved with human trafficking and he is looking for Angelica, the mother of my Carlitos." Carlos paced the floor as if someone was right outside the door waiting for him to come out.

"Simple. Marry her and make her legal," explained Diego.

Carlos paused for a moment and stopped pacing, "Well, we are already married. But that doesn't matter to El Coyote. As far as he is concerned, Angelica is his property."

"How much do you think it will take for Espinoza to leave Angelica in peace?" asked Diego, knowing that to coyotes it was a matter of money. These workers that he supplied to farmers and retailers were his slaves, his property, and he expected to be compensated for their labor.

"I don't know, but I will tell you this, these pinche garlic farmers knowingly hire many of the coyote's workers and pay them less than minimum to pick their garlic," Carlos raised his angry voice so loud that he woke up Chi. She went into the kitchen and brewed some tea and brought three cups on a tray. The two friends continued talking about his hide-and-seek life to keep Angelica two steps ahead of her coyote.

A lifetime seemed to go by as Carlos and Diego shared common experiences with Chi: their secret hideouts as children, the altars they had built, and the names of their club: The Hoppers; Tamalero, Chinito, and Smiley. She encouraged Carlos to bring his family to visit them at their Berkeley cottage. Diego knew that Carlos would not visit again, least of all with his family, but he knew that from then on they would keep in contact by phone. Carlos left as the sun was beginning to peek over the Oakland hills.

Two months later, League of United Latin American Citizens (LULAC) filled an unfair labor suit against twenty merchants from the San Francisco Bay Area down to Hollister, California for working their employees more than 60-80 hours a week and paying them for only 40 hours at minimum wage. Since the Garlic Festival Committee members were the biggest donors and there was likely to be a smaller profit margin than in previous years because of increased labor costs, there would be fewer dollars for the non-profit organizations than in past years, even though they were still predicting the sale of over ten tons of beef, four tons of pasta, and two tons of garlic at the garlic festival.

The year passed with no progress on catching SKK. In fact, it seemed that many law enforcement officers cared less and less about catching him. SKK was doing a better job of catching criminals than the police departments in the Bay Area. Among the many police departments in the Bay Area, SKK had become a cult hero. From Diego's standpoint, two relevant facts concerning SKK surfaced from the festival: learning that Marconi Wines sponsored both the Garlic Festival and wine tasting events at the Claremont and that Stanley Marconi had been at both events. The investigation also revealed that many of the businessmen that frequented the Claremont Hotel attended the Garlic Festival on an annual basis. Stanley Marconi was one of fifty people who were connected to both the Claremont Hotel and the Garlic Festival.

Carlos called Diego and invited him and Chi to visit with his family at Crissy Field Park, near the Fisherman's Wharf. The park had a spectacular view of Golden Gate Bridge. Chi had prepared a picnic basket with bread, cheese, fruit, and a bottle of wine. Carlos took a blanket and spread it on the beach for Carlitos to lie on. He was so sound asleep that not even an earthquake would wake him. Diego went to his car to pick up a football that he had in the trunk of his car, when he noticed someone in Carlos's car. With the football being tossed from one hand to the other, Diego asked, *"Who's in your car?"*

"Angelica is frightened of the possibility that El Coyote will apprehend her and turn her over to immigration or worse," replied Carlos sadly. *"She won't come out. She's also embarrassed that she does not speak English well enough to be sociable."*

Chi stood up and walked to the car. She opened the door and stepped into the car and sat on the driver's side of the car. Diego threw the football away from Carlos so that he would have to run to catch it. He managed to finally catch the ball after tipping into the air and then controlling it. They threw the ball around until Carlitos woke up and required attention. Chi and Angelica stepped out of the car and walked over to Carlitos. Chi helped Angelica cover while she breast-fed Carlitos. Carlos and Diego sat down on the sand and enjoyed a glass of wine while the women looked after Carlitos' needs.

"How is Rosa?" asked Diego with the violent fragmented images of his father and Rosa still floating in his mind.

"She is not well," Carlos sadly replied. "She is in and out of the hospital. Her body is giving up. She has everything: heart, stomach, and back problems, not to mention dementia. Sometimes she doesn't recognize me." Carlos' eyes watered. They preferred talking about their membership in the Hoppers than the current situation. The stories of hideouts and secret signals brought the needed levity to their day. Chi walked Angélina and the baby to where Carlos and Diego were deep in nostalgia.

"Pobrecita mi Rosita," said Angelica covering her eyes and crying into her hands."

Then, looking at Chi, she whispered to Carlos: *"Chi se mira como los Indios de Oaxaca, los Zapotecos!"*

"Yes, that is true, Chi looks like the Zapotecs from Oaxaca," interpreted Carlos for Chi even though she was fluent in Spanish.

"Angelica understands much more English than she can speak," defended Carlos.

"I am sorry to hear about your mother Carlos," interjected Chi. *"Diego speaks very highly of your mother."*

Seeing Carlos' eyes water up slightly, Diego placed his arm on Carlos' shoulders and changed the subject to another problematic one: *"Well, what is the latest about El Coyote?"*

Carlos' emotions shifted, replacing sadness with hate, and his lungs filled with rage and uttered broken syllables, making the words hard to understand, *"I wiiiill kiiilll that son of a bitch!"*

"Don't ever speak like that, Carlos," warned Chi. She looked over at Diego, upset that he had even brought up the subject.

"Don't you know, at least twenty of his mojados, undocumented workers, have been found butchered in the fields between Watsonville and Hollister?" spat Carlos.

Diego noticed that Chi and Angelica were deep in conversation. He was really impressed with Chi's linguistic abilities, a truly cross-cultural Chinita. They continued speaking to each other and occasionally laughing at one thing or another. Diego and Carlos were busy sharing criminal information on homicide victims. Carlos was certain that El Coyote was behind the killing of the undocumented migrant workers. Besides homeless people, and women in general, undocumented immigrants were certainly among the most vulnerable victims in society. These homicides were not thoroughly investigated; most of these cases were closed without being investigated. Law enforcement certainly had their priorities and finding justice for undocumented workers had never been one of them.

Diego and Carlos visited several more times that year before the next Garlic Festival. Diego and Chi had been involved in at least twenty homicides between the two of them before being assigned undercover to attend the festival. They were not looking forward to the long lines in the blistering sun. The sweat rolled down their faces as they drank water, and soft drinks. The garlic-flavored food was out of this world. They stuffed their faces with garlic fries as they visited the booths. The three days were without incident, the extra security was certainly evident everywhere, both uniformed and undercover.

By the third year of FBI surveillance of the Gilroy Garlic Festival that Diego and Chi attended, security was visibly less than in previous years. The festival committee felt that the additional heightened security had kept some way, and local law enforcement agencies had difficulty justifying the expense of maintaining their presence at such high levels. Consequently, security was significantly reduced. However, 4,000 volunteers assisted with parking, shuttle service, admissions, and as servers at Gourmet Alley. Chi noted that many of the garlic farmers were patrolling the grounds with their cell phones. It seems that farmers and merchants were more involved than in previous years with the overall operations of the entire festival.

The first day of each festival is dedicated to the locals from Gilroy, San Martín, San Juan Bautista, Hollister, and Morgan Hill, who get a $5 discount on their admission. How wonderful for a whole community to have a festival where they can meet all their friends and celebrate "community." The Garlic Festival is like having a community-wide reunion on an annual basis. The locals do not mind the hot temperatures, the long lines, and the pungent smell of garlic.

On the next morning, Diego's cell buzzed at 4:13am, *"Yes, Captain Williams, I am awake now."*

"SKK struck again at the Garlic Festival as we thought he would. Get down there as soon as you can," ordered Captain Williams.

Diego turned on the lights, but not the siren to his police car as he raced to Christmas Hill Park. The night was beginning to lose its fight with the sunrise. It was still dark when Diego drove up next to a squad of police cars shining their police car lights at the amphitheater where officers inspected the crime scene. Immediately after stepping out of the car, Diego sensed a strong presence in the air; someone was watching him.

Captain Williams called out, *"We have a victim hanging from the rafters by his wrists and ankles."* The limbs were stretched out like those in Leonardo da Vinci's drawing, The Vitruvian Man.

Diego stood in silence while he studied the hideous crime scene. He prayed, "In the presence of our enemies, we will fear not evil. For the Lord is with us...."

"Someone has taken a lot of time to decorate this crime scene, and execute this homicide," declared Diego at first glance. The victim, who appeared to be of Mexican ancestry, was naked and suspended in a spider web of ropes. The victim's wrists and ankles were tied; his chin rested on its chest. Hundreds of dollar bills were stuffed in his mouth and up his anus. There were no apparent wounds on the body. The body would have to be taken down and examined before determining cause of death. The body continued hanging for the next hour, while the detectives and forensics inspected the crime scene and seized evidence for further review by the forensics lab technicians.

The wall behind the hanging victim had green letters that were three feet tall that read "El Coyote." Diego immediately remembered Carlos' threat to kill El Coyote, *"I willll kiilll him!"* Diego shelved Carlos' words and continued to analyze the crime scene: a large altar was constructed at the foot of the El Coyote sign and the hanging victim. SKK's signature was all over the crime scene: lots of candles, a funerary urn, which appeared to be a piece from Bo Nianzu's collection, postcards with Catholic saints, and a small statue of the La Virgen de Guadalupe. The scent of burning wax, lavender and copal permeated the air in Christmas Hill Park. The police allowed the candles and incense to burn. However, they did put out the fire burning Nianzu's funerary art to preserve the evidence. The artifact was a key piece of evidence. This was clearly the "the burning of paper," or Dzidzat, the ritual in memory of those that have passed. The artifact was put out in time to preserve the whole structure, but someone would have to read and extrapolate the hidden meaning behind Nianzu's art piece. FBI and law enforcement from the Bay Area would look to Nianzu to shed light in the investigation of this case.

Captain Williams informed Diego that the security guards were sleeping when the police car spotted the fire at the amphitheater. The police officer on patrol immediately put out the fire. He did not find any blood in the area. He had discovered the sleeping guards at different places of Christmas Hill Park. They had been served Somabien, sleeping pills, in their coffee.

"Do we know who provided the coffee?" asked Diego.

"No! But we are looking into it right now!" Williams replied.

After the Gilroy Police Chief arrived, his officers instantaneously started yellow taping the crime scene. At the feet of the victim, the officers found scattered pictures of other homicide victims, all farm workers: older men, young women, and children. All of them were butchered, with their guts hanging out from their stomachs, a sure way to instill fear in other farm workers. As in previous SKK crime scenes, the photos, newspaper articles about these mysterious deaths, and weapons linked the hanging victim to a series of farm worker homicides. This time, personal items such as keys, clothing, glasses, and driver licenses belonging to the farm worker victims were piled up directly under the hanging victim's feet. Adding to this evidence, officers later located two Gilroy police files involving a man identified by some migrant workers as Julio Cortez, "El Coyote." He was interrogated about the farm worker homicides, but farmers said he was an honest labor contractor, and he was released.

As Diego read the police files, thoughts of corruption in city government and among the community's most powerful businessmen floated about in his mind. Perhaps the respectable pillars of the community were using El Coyote to generate a ready supply of undocumented farm workers who would work for subminimum wages so the farmers could sustain their high profit margin and maintain their prosperity? A selected group of rich and influential persons could be responsible for the protection of farm labor contractors like Julio Cortez. Diego decided that these individuals also had to be flushed out so that the work of all the honest people involved with the Garlic Festival would not be stained with blood; after all, the festival profits have contributed approximately ten million dollars to local non-profit organizations and have funded major improvements in the community.

The police and security had taped off, put up fences, and installed barriers completely around the amphitheater by the time the sun came out. The Gilroy Dispatch cited "structural repairs of the amphitheater" as the reason for its closure. The Chief of the Gilroy Police Department, as well as Captain Williams, and the FBI agreed to conceal the homicide for the third day of the festival. Thirty security guards in their navy blue uniforms surrounded the amphitheater for the entire day.

Diego was about to go to the car when his cellphone buzzed, *"Yes, this is Detective de Campos."*

"Diego, this is Carlos," he sounded rather anxious and out of breathe.

"I was just going to call you," answered Diego as he lowered his voice so that no one could hear him.

"I just got a call that El Coyote has been killed," said Carlos, *"is that true?"*

"And how did you find out, Carlos?" asked Diego.

"I received a call from one of the security guards," answered Carlos. *"I didn't do it, if that's what you were thinking."*

"Well, you are right, I was thinking that you killed him. Buddy, you better have a good alibi," said Diego.

"No, I didn't kill him, but I'm damned glad he's dead,"

volunteered Carlos with frankness. *"Is Chi with you?"*

"No she's home," answered Diego reluctantly. *"We'll visit later, I am at the crime scene. Hey, do you know anything about the Chinese funerary structures that was found at the altar at the crime scene?"* asked Diego, still fishing for clues of a possible connection.

"What are you talking about? What funerary structures?" asked Carlos?

Diego was relieved with Carlos' answer. He thought about the other crime scenes and remembered the clues that SKK left, pointing to the location of the next killing. After a little more fishing for clues questions, he terminated the conversation with Carlos and ran back to the crime scene. He ducked under the yellow tape and looked about the altar until he found what he was looking for, the clue to when the next homicide would take place. A new Oakland Raider's baseball cap was resting on the head of a statue of Buddha. He reached in his coat pocket, pulled out a latex glove, and forced his right hand into the glove. He reached down to grab the baseball cap. He examined the cap and found the number 12 sewed on the inside lining of the cap.

Chapter 11

Rosales, Rose Bushes

Rosales

In order for roses and women to blossom, they require a great deal of attention. Beautiful rosebushes do not care for themselves. A rosebush will live through the most unfavorable conditions; the result of such neglect is muted rosebuds that don't open, and the petals get infested with aphids. Nonetheless, through all the neglect, rosebushes somehow manage to live on. On the other hand, if it is pruned at the right angle before spring, fertilized before the first bloom and after each blossom, generously skirted with mulch, and watered deep and consistently, the bush will yield a sunshine of smiling red, yellow, coral, purple, pink and white roses. Some rosebuds start out red, and later when they open up, they stretch out in shades of pink and sometimes yellow. And if you are lucky, the sunlight will enter and travel through the translucent petals to showcase a full spectrum of colors.

Rosa Santos

She dreams of herself in a black graduation cap and gown and marching slowly with a diploma from Harvard Law School in hand. She desperately looks about for Juan Carlos in the crowd of happy faces. His handsome face looks about, too, craning his neck and chin for a better view of Rosa. His eyes finally get a glimpse of her and Juan Carlos' face beams in complete bliss. With outstretched arms, they begin to run towards each other, they embrace, kissing madly in the middle of a crowd. The volume of the peoples' voices and laughter reduces itself noticeably and the images of people's faces begin to fade. Rosa and Juan Carlos' smiling faces stay in focus while the others dissipate into a white mist.

Rosa woke up with a smile on her face, partly due to the oral sex she had with Juan Carlos, but also because she had found herself reliving her childhood dream of becoming a lawyer, when everyone recognized her potential, and everything seemed possible. It was such a crazy dream, but she loved remembering it. Her present lot in life...Juan Carlos arrived home from Viet Nam. Nonetheless She was just happy to have him back and to be able to continue to love him in so many ways, limited as they were. She was sensitized to not treat Juan Carlos as a cripple. His war injuries left him impotent, and it castrated his self-esteem. He was on his own self-proclaimed exile from his true love, Rosa. His condition really troubled him, remembering how much she liked sex. How wrong it felt to deny her the sweet gifts of happiness and pleasure, and to be trapped in this inescapable human tragedy. Juan Carlos loved Rosa, but was afraid that he would not be enough of a man to love her.

Rosa hurried to nurse Carlitos and help him back to sleep before attending to Juan Carlos. A deliveryman dropped off beer, soda, bottled water, hard liquor and cigarettes. The commodities were all put away before Juan Carlos stirred to signal that he was awake. He sat on the bed while he reached for his legs and started putting them on when Rosa entered the room. She looked so lovely, with wavy long brown hair, a touch of make-up, and red lipstick. She looked as pretty as the woman on the classic Mexican movies. She was ready to be kissed a hundred times, but Juan Carlos was not clean yet and pushed her away and headed for the shower. Rosa expected a hug and a kiss before the start of the day, and after last night's lovemaking, it didn't matter how clean his kiss tasted. The kiss didn't come; instead Juan Carlos closed down and went into his wounded veteran's protective shell. Rosa noticed his distance all morning; she nonetheless sang some of his favorite songs to see if that would change his mood.

Any response was better than being shunned, as far as Rosa was concerned, so she tried her best to lift his mood. Unfortunately, the singing had no effect on his current state of mind. He brooded as he cleaned the bar over and over again, as if having a shiny clean bar was the most important thing in the world. Rosa worked around the kitchen at the back of the bar; watching Juan Carlos to see if he gave any signs that he was now approachable.

"Any request?" asked Rosa, attempting to reach out and perhaps draw a response.

"Sing any song, I like'em all," a small ray of light escaped his guarded heart.

"Like'em all," Rosa echoed the words as if in a song.

Rosa's Cantina went through some renovations; a new billboard read *Rosa's Hot Tamales* and a ramp was built next to the register and bar so that Juan Carlos could maneuver his new electric wheelchair. He could now decide if he should walk or just ride. Riding became the preferred mode of transportation. The wheelchair was so manageable that it could spin in circles with little effort. Juan Carlos perched himself behind the cash register and from there he could reign over his cantina. Weeks passed as if they were days and the months ate up a whole year before Juan Carlos noticed that Rosales' Cantina was making a pretty good profit.

Rosa sang and danced for the customers while she served them drinks and food. Juan Carlos bought her some Mexican faldas for the dancing on Friday and Saturday nights. The skirts really added to her dancing routines of Guadalajara, Adelita, and other songs. Rosa had fun as bartender-server-dancer and made the performance into an art. People came to Rosa's to interact with her. She handled people so swiftly that you could love her and be concerned about your safety at the same time. *"¡Cuidaté! Watch yourself!"* she warned anyone who entered her guarded space. Otherwise, Rosa would make them laugh, sometimes at themselves.

At the start of the second year of Rosa's Cantina, a company truck delivered a big shiny jukebox. Juan Carlos had secretly purchased some of Rosa's favorite records: José Alfredo Jiménez, Javier Solís, Flaco Jiménez, Luis Miguel, José Feliciano, Linda Ronstadt and many more.

"Gracias por la Caja de Música," Rosa expressed herself with a warm smile. *"Now I can sing along and dance for you!"*

"Don't mention it, really it was nothing," Juan Carlos sadly answered.

Rosa looked for her favorite Mexican female singer, Ana Gabriel; she found her and pressed start. *"Luna, tú que lo vez, Luna, tú que sabes donde está, díle que lo quiero - Moon, you who can see him, tell him I love him,"* she echoed the song in English. *"Te dí una parte de mi, te dí una parte de mi, te dí lo que pude y algo mas. I have given you a part of me, I gave you all of me and then some more."*

Every morning from that day forward, the happy Mexican music would wake up Juan Carlos and Carlitos. Rosa headed directly to Juan Carlos to thank him again, but he just brushed her off as if to gesture that the jukebox was a business investment.

Carlitos enjoyed music and his mother's singing. *"Ay, yi, yi, yi, canto y no lloro,"* sang Carlitos as he stepped into the car that drove him to preschool, all the while Rosa planting tens of kisses all over his face.

"¡Te quiero, te quiero, mi amor!" Rosa gave so much love to Carlitos, it could have filled a hand basket, *"I love you too much!"* Carlitos felt a special bond with Rosa, who always hugged and kissed him. He knew how it felt to be loved by his mother.

Rosa's Cantina became popular with the campesinos from the southern side of Gilroy. Rosa's singing and dancing had weekend draws that exceeded their business capacity of thirty people. Rosa sang and danced solos throughout the evening while bartending. Juan Carlos hired a young woman to serve a limited menu of tamales, frijoles, chili, and cocido, a delicious meat soup with vegetables. Rosa's hot tamales sold before they were made, people placed their orders. The orders of tamales that were not picked up were either sold at the cantina or delivered by Carlitos to those living in the Conejeras.

"Octavio, que lástima que se van a morir los feos!" teased one drunk to another, *"Yeah, how sad that all the ugly people are gonna die and it's been nice knowing you!"*

"¡Adios, compadre, tú eres más feo que yo!" another drunk added "And you my friend are uglier than I," as the men continued verbally jousting and laughing at each other.

All in all, Rosa's Cantina was flourishing and becoming a local attraction and so were Juan Carlos and Rosa. Speaking of notoriety, both had gained about twenty pounds since the cantina opened for business. For Juan Carlos, the weight gain had begun when he preferred to ride the wheelchair rather than struggle walking with his prosthetic legs. For Rosa, it was Juan Carlos not demonstrating his love for her. Since his return from Viet Nam,

Rosa had dolled herself up for him. She sang and danced for him and yet he did not show that he loved her back. Juan Carlos avoided touching her in any way. In fact, he no longer said anything when attempts to grab Rosa were made by some of the drunks. Rosa was a strong, firm, and tall woman at the prime of her life and she was giving all of herself to be with the man she loved. *Life was so unfair,* she thought.

"Felicidades por haber roto mi corazón en mil pedazos," sang Rosa welling to tears and feeling broken into a thousand pieces. *"Gracias por haberte conocido,"* she continued singing in the kitchen, *"thank you for letting me get to know you."*

Rosa's need for physical contact became evident while she danced. She became more sexually expressive with her movements, bringing the men's animal instincts to the surface. Before long, the men had to be scraped from the ceiling or splashed with a bucket of cold water to shock them back to civility. Heated passion filled the already heavy air; to calm the savage beast, some of those men who left the cantina drunk and horny looked to hire a prostitute for the night. Rosa swayed her arms above her head in the opposite rhythm than the rest of her body, and then suddenly she'd hold her arms still while the body swayed side to side like a snake. Rosa felt like coming out of her body and leaving this world, and she would do so, if not for Carlitos. The thought of abandoning Carlos passed through her body like a cold chill.

"Rosa, an army buddy of mine is coming over for a visit this weekend," warned Juan Carlos not knowing his friend's current mental condition, as he wiped the bar counter over and over again. *"He might not be all in one piece since Vietnam, but he sounded all right on the phone."* Before long, Sargent Lonnie García was knocking on the door.

"JC! Are you in here?" hollered Lonnie, as he opened the door and walked in.

"Sorry, we aren't open!" yelled Juan Carlos when he heard someone at the door.

Lonnie wore his army uniform when he visited with Juan Carlos. Lonnie took two steps into Rosa's Cantina and noticed a fat JC in a wheelchair. Lonnie got choked up and felt a sense of melancholy weigh heavily on his heart as he stared at JC, who had once been an amazing athlete, now reduced to a crippled man in a wheelchair.

Juan Carlos also felt melancholy, something he had not done in front of Rosa. He had always tried to hold his heart in check, but with Lonnie, he could let it out. They had both been through hell and back, they sustained physical and emotional trauma. Rosa could not imagine what these two men had been through in the war. Rosa pieced together the bits of Lonnie's stories and concluded that he was having difficulty with having killed helpless women and children for reasons he now considered unjustifiable.

That evening Rosa also handled the cash register besides bartending. Somehow, Margarita, the new server was able to manage more than the usual busy night. Rosa attempted to have them talk about something else besides the woes of war, so she delivered a large plate of tamales and Charro **(whole)** beans to Juan Carlos and Lonnie, seated in the cantina's only booth. Seven years had passed since their return from Vietnam, but in many ways it seemed that they left part of themselves over there. Lonnie fell asleep in the booth. Rosa helped him to his feet and walked him into her bedroom in the Conejera. Rosa picked up the loose plates and glasses before helping Juan Carlos to his bedroom in the cantina. Expectantly, Juan Carlos tapped Rosa's arm, signaling her to go to be with Lonnie, so she slipped into her bed with her husband's war buddy. Sometime during the night, Lonnie smelled Rosa's scent, stimulating him and allowing his hands to travel in her direction. When he touched Rosa, a stimulus response sent waves of pleasure throughout her body. She was on fire. Lonnie looked at Rosa for approval to proceed. Rosa's answer was to kiss Lonnie passionately as if he was Juan Carlos. In the cantina's bedroom, Juan Carlos stirred with discomfort from drinking too much, vomited in the bathroom, and crawled to get back to his bed. Lonnie and Rosa stayed up, and continued their discussion of the war and the trouble he was having with the reality that he had killed soldiers, civilians, women and children. Lonnie opened up about what was troubling him. They talked for about two hours before having sex again. Rosa climbed on top of Lonnie and rode him in a delicious salsa rhythm.

The next morning, Rosa, Juan Carlos, and Lonnie had huevos rancheros and coffee for breakfast. Lonnie, still wearing his uniform, was finally wearing a smile on his face. Rosa didn't know how to react, she carefully watched Juan Carlos for any clues on how he felt. Juan Carlos knew how Rosa felt, by mid-day, Rosa was singing like a jukebox: one song after another, without breaks, performing on her inner stage.

"JC, you have been a true soul brother for letting me stay over last night. I've been going through hell and back, dealing with the guilt of having killed so many people. I had to regurgitate all the venom caused by war. Rosa talked me through some troubled waters and I thank you both for that. I am feeling a lot better about myself," Lonnie honestly expressed his gratitude.

Rosa did not want to take credit for Lonnie's wellness and said, *"We all have our medicine that we take to cure our ills, that is, those of us that want to feel better about the life we're living."*

Rosa walked over to Juan Carlos and kissed him on the top of his head without saying a word. For just a moment, he let down his guard and permitted her to be close enough to display some affection; something that Rosa was willing to show on invitation. Rosa always carefully protected his manhood by waiting for a smile, an accidental touch, or some other invitation before she expressed any physical affection toward him. Juan Carlos never mentioned Lonnie's rendezvous with Rosa again. While Juan Carlos did not become as loving as before, he did become friendlier and more considerate towards Rosa.

One late Saturday night, a drunk finally broke the silence and solicited sex with Rosa, *"Fifty dollars for a night in my car?"*

"You go downtown for the twenty dollar putas!" laughed Rosa with indignation. *"To touch me costs $500, but I wouldn't let you touch*

me for a million!" She waved off the poor fool. Drunks who had enjoyed her dancing dreamed of saving enough money to someday taste the likes of Rosa. By the weekend, the word spread that it would take $500 to fuck Rosa. One night Rosa heard a knock on her door.

"*¡Quién es?* Rosa asked, "*Who's there?"*

"*¡Quinientos dolares!"* answered a man with $500 dollars.

"*¡Espera!"* Rosa asked him to wait. She made a bed for Carlitos in the closet and carried him into it. She opened the door, and from that day forward, the campesinos occasionally skipped sending a monthly check to their families in México. The clandestine rendezvous became such a frequent occurrence that it was public knowledge that for $500, one could spend the night with Rosa. Carlitos had a few fights to protect his mother's name and reputation in third grade, but after a few years, it seemed that people accepted Rosa Santos's profession. Everyone liked Rosa; she was a jubilant person who was friendly, funny, and intelligent.

Juan Carlos had a two by four inch one-way window inserted on the wall between his bedroom and Rosa's bedroom. Through the window, Juan Carlos claimed he could watch out for Rosa and burst in her bedroom with a gun if necessary. Rosa had no knowledge of the gun. Perhaps at first, the window was to protect Rosa, but after several encounters, the watching through the one-way window became perverted, Juan Carlos pretended that he was the man making love with Rosa.

One warm evening, before the sun went behind the tall walnut trees, Carlitos brought his best friend, Diego to spend Saturday night over in his secret hideout. Rosa did not walk into the bedroom until 1 am. Diego and Carlitos had fallen asleep in the closet. Rosa did not know Diego was sleeping over. The boys were awakened by noises coming from the banging of the bed against the wall.

"You must never tell anyone what you are about to see, promise?" demanded Carlitos.

"I promise!" Diego gave his word.

Diego opened the swiveled closet shutters. The shutters were adjustable and they could be opened to allow more air into the closet to ventilate the clothes. Carlos opened them for more visibility of the bedroom. Diego opened the shutters a little without making a sound. At first, he noticed a man on top of Rosa slamming his body against her and she seemed to enjoy it by thrusting her hips against his body. Diego began to sweat profusely and blinked his eyes to see more clearly through the opened panels. Carlitos had seen his mother beaten so many times on Saturday night that he was desensitized and accustom to seeing his mother with bruises on her face. What Diego was about to see would traumatize him for the rest of his life; he noticed that the man fighting with Rosa had a tattoo of a rose on his shoulder like his father, Don Robo. It was Don Robo fighting with Rosa. Suddenly, Don Robo started slapping Rosa and then punching her. Rosa's face was bloodied with the slap and after the second punch, blood spluttered on the sheets, the floor, and the walls. The splattered blood was not only Rosa's. Rosa was not shy or scared; she punched him right back. She grabbed his boot from under the bed and began beating Don Robo on the head with his own boot. The heel of the boot struck him in the eye and instantly, it started bleeding. Diego wanted to open the closet door and stop the fight, but he had promised not to interfere with activity in the bedroom, and he was terrified of what would happen if his father knew he was watching."

"So you think you're big shot?" asked Rosa. *"Uh? You're just like any little man, acting like a big man. Don't you know that the dog that barks the loudest is the one that is most afraid!"*

"Cállate! Shut the fuck up, you bitch," cursed Don Robo.

"I am not a Bitch, pendejo!" Rosa exclaimed. She knew that Don Robo needed to get angry to purge the poison from his soul.

135

They slapped and punched each other a few more times before having sex again. Don Robo swore at his life, and the degradation he had to endure, he swore at his father for leaving the family. Rosa pointed out to Don Robo that many farm workers' children grew up without fathers and they accepted it: Mexican men were working as braceros in the US while their families lived in México. The nearby community knew Rosa as the man-handler. She could take men's punches and give them right back and somehow still end up in on friendly terms with them. Everybody liked Rosa Santos.

Later, Rosario nursed her husband's eye and badly bruised face with wet cold towels. And once that was done, Rosario visited Rosa to stitch her bottom lip together. She inserted the needle and thread into Rosa's lip, drawing streams of tears from eyes. Rosa's face did not look as bad as Don Robo's, but her black eyes were starting to swell. She was surprised that Carlitos had not woken up with the loud noises from the fight, not knowing that Diego had witnessed his best friend's mother get brutalized by his father.

Rosalinda Mercado

As the sun was about to hide behind the tall walnut trees, a 55 Chevy loaded with people and their belongings parked in front of the only two-story house on Rosanna Street and next to the driveway of what the Gilroy community named Bracero Lane, the entrance of the Conejeras.

The smell of hot fresh blood filled the car. Rosalinda Mercado in the back seat was in the middle of a miscarriage. The children cried for Juan, their father to drive to a hospital.

"Don Juan, please find a hospital!" they begged.

"You want to see me go to jail? Who will feed you, pendejos?" Juan regretted having to take care of this undeserving family.

"He's right, at the hospital, they'll ask too many questions and throw your father in jail," whimpered Rosalinda. Her body slowly expelled the fetus, the lifeless body lay there in a puddle of blood. Rosalinda still had some afterbirth coming out. Throughout all this pain, she still did not cry.

The lights on the porch of the two-story house came on and a man dressed in black came out pointing a flashlight at them. *"Car trouble?"* asked a man with a strange accent.

"No, my mother is bleeding to death!" alerted Coca, the youngest of the kids.

"Hospital, four blocks straight ahead, two right!" said the Chinese man.

"No, hospital, hospital brings the police and if they come there will be lots of trouble," answered Don Juan with the same intonation as the man in black. He paced back and forth beside the car.

"*Let me see?*" the Asian man asked permission to get a better look. He flashed the light at Rosalinda's midsection, and between the legs where the little body laid still. He then shined the light on Rosalinda's face and immediately became alarmed at this life or death situation. Since they were not going to drive her to the hospital or call for an ambulance, he had no other recourse but to bring Rosalinda into his bedroom, which was on the first floor. All the other bedrooms were on the second floor.

"My name is Yiwu!" He immediately took matters into his own hands. Yiwu was focused on saving Rosalinda's life. He boiled water with herbs, poured them into a towel, and placed the hot towel on Rosalinda's vagina. After Rosalinda rested in his bed, Coca, the only girl in the family cleaned as much blood off without taking off Rosalinda's skirt. After giving her family a moment to visit, Yiwu ordered everyone out of the room or he would call the police. Everyone walked out and waited by the 55 Chevy.

"*Rosalinda, your name. Yes?*"

"*Yes, Rosalinda. And yours?*" asked Rosalinda.

Yiwu Yungfu said his name in Chinese and Rosalinda was not able to hear the sounds clearly enough to repeat his name. After several fruitless attempts, she finally said, "*I will call you Mi Chinito!*" half smiling at him. "*My baby is dead, yes?*"

"*Yes,*" said Yiwu with so much sadness in his face.

"*Yes, I must clean and sterilize instruments to doctor you, Ok?*" asked Yiwu with a bow.

"*I am going to remove your bloody clothes and wrap this sheet around you.*" He swiftly removed all her clothes, washed her body with warm wet towels, and dried her with thick cotton towels. A cup of Long Jing Green Tea was given to Rosalinda. Her face grimaced as she drank the tea. The thick towel she was sitting on filled with blood and more afterbirth. The towel was replaced with a warm wet one. Again, she was exposed as Yiwu cleaned her and wrapped her in white silk. She fell asleep after three hours of sweating and enduring sharp jolts of pain. Yiwu cleaned the room, tightly wrapped the lifeless little bundle in a white sheet and walked out of the house. After he returned, Rosalinda told Yiwu she had named her dead son, Popocatepetl, after one of the volcanoes near Pueblo, México. For short, she would refer to him as "Popo!" She rested alone in her room, thinking of her life and the direction it was taking. Don Juan will always be an angry man needing someone to take out his frustration on and most often; she was his unfortunate punching bag. After Yiwu's disappearance into the dark of night, no one ever talked about "Popo", Rosalinda's dead son.

Late in the afternoon, Yiwu walked out of the bedroom and invited everyone to come in for a short visit with Rosalinda and asked everyone to be very quiet and not waken her. The children exaggerated the quiet steps, and tiptoed around the bed where she was sleeping. The three children clasped their hands together and prayed, but Don Juan could not look down at Rosalinda. After five minutes, Yiwu came back and asked everyone to let Rosalinda rest. Juan took one of the bedrooms upstairs and the three children shared the other room. Yiwu slept on a chair beside a sleeping Rosalinda.

Rosalinda woke up to Yiwu's smiling face. *"Good morning Rosalinda, green tea from China, drink!"* he demanded in a gentle manner with concern.

In all of Rosalinda's life, she had not experienced such kindness and respect. Always dressed in black, he approached with the necessary medication for the day. Nursing Rosalinda required around the clock care: high fever, vomiting, and a worrisome lack of appetite persisted for days. About the second week, Rosalinda started showing signs of recovery: she was eating more, drinking water and tea with regularity. Her face and mood seemed tired and withdrawn, perhaps from looking death right in the eye and deciding to come back for a chance at happiness.

"Buenos Dias, Rosalinda! Here a linda rosa", exclaimed Yiwu with a smiling face and closed eyes as he handed her a yellow rose. *"Roses are as lovely as you!"* said Yiwu. And so, Rosalinda woke up a smiling face and to a freshly cut rose. *"You look at the rose, then look at yourself in the mirror, then look at the rose and look at yourself in the mirror, same beauty,"* says Yiwu with a nod of his head. *"Smell the roses, Rosalinda!"*

"Oh, gracias Mi Chinito por tu cariño," Rosalinda expressed her gratitude. At times, she looked forward to spending time with him more than visiting with her family. She certainly didn't look forward to visiting with Juan. He was always angry and hustling for another auto repair job. In the last three years, he had not expressed any kindness. Don Juan and the kids worked on cars and Rosalinda took care of everything else. She did not have time to smell the roses.

"You are feeling better, yes?" asked Yiwu handing her a pink rose to smell its sweet aroma.

"Yes and thanks to you for saving my life," Rosalinda grabbed his hand and held on to it. She squeezed his hand in hers and thanked him while looking right into his eyes. Since Rosalinda came into his life, an unknown world with love in it seemed to open before him. He was falling in love with Rosalinda and he was unable to hide his feeling from her. A day did not pass without him showing in a small way his love for her, and most frequently with a bouquet of roses. They would both smell them and laugh. Rosalinda returned her affection to her Mi Chinito. She would openly say that she would not take another breath of fresh air if it had not been for her Chinito's care, he saved her life and Don Juan's brutal assault caused the internal bleeding which induced the miscarriage.

One morning, while Yiwu stepped out to buy some breakfast supplies, Rosalinda put some light makeup, eye shadow, and lipstick on before he returned. When she opened her eyes, his round face was not smiling. Rosalinda was as beautiful as the lavender roses he was giving her. *"You're prettier than the roses,"* Yiwu had difficulty speaking, he stuttered as he shared his feelings. Rosalinda was ready to return to her family full time. One day, Rosalinda woke up to a bed full of red roses; this was the day Rosalinda cried because she realized that she had never been loved with so much kindness.

"You will always be Mi Chinito, mi amor!" she said to him with a kiss on the lips.

The day that Rosalinda moved into the bedroom upstairs with Don Juan was the day her face took on a permanent frown. This was also the time Yiwu realized that he had lost control of the situation: Don Juan was working on four cars in the backyard and also across the alley, in the empty lot next to the Ice Cream Company. He and his kids were working on cars: Coca was bent over under the hood of one car, while Juanito's legs were sticking out from underneath another car. There was no shortage of work at Don Juan's Auto Repair Shop.

When he wasn't working on cars, he was either yelling at Rosalinda or the kids. To avoid the noise pollution, Yiwu escaped to a bed he had prepared in the shed. He cringed when he thought of his most fervent desire, to kick Don Juan on the head and putting him out of miserable life. One early morning, he ran into Rosalinda in the kitchen and noticed a blackened eye. He was so infuriated that he promised himself that he would kill Don Juan. Rosalinda noticed how upset Yiwu had become and approached him to say, *"He knows I don't love him any longer and he blames you."*

"I should kill him for hurting you again!" Yiwu's face turned red, the veins on his neck and forehead inflated with blood.

"He will never have my heart again, my heart belongs to you, Mi Chinito." She kissed him on his forehead. *"Mi Chinito, mi amor! I will always love you."* Rosalinda cried in silence and kissed him while he cried, too.

Don Juan and the children worked hard to save enough

money to leave Yiwu's house, but the total savings never really amounted to enough to sustain a family of five for more than two months. Don Juan knocked on the door of the shed, where Yiwu was mediating.

"Chinaman, come out! I want to talk to you!" he demanded.

Yiwu was in some distant planet or a space where the banging on the door was muted by the serenity of an elevated state. The banging and yelling continued until he opened his mind and heard the banging. He was sitting on the bamboo carpet and he slowly stood up while the banging steadily continued. *"What is it?"* he asked as if forcing the air in his lungs to release the words.

"Rosalinda is different, what did you do? What did you say to her?" insisted Don Juan.

"It is your black heart that poisoned her. What really happened to her before you arrived at my front door? You killed your child and you almost killed Rosalinda too!" Yiwu Yungfu stood very erect and motionless; only his lips moved. *"You must leave my house!"* he demanded.

The thought of having to leave the house disarmed Don Juan's threat to accost Yiwu in any way. His desperate financial situation governed his pride and asked for reconsideration. *"We do not have enough money to find another place to live at this time!"*

"Ok, you can stay two more months but you can't hit Rosalinda or your kids anymore," Yiwu insisted on this condition for a settlement. *"If you physically abuse your wife or kids, you go. Agree?"* he insisted.

"Agree! Thank you, but you must stay away from Rosalinda," Don Juan added a condition of his own to the agreement.

The Mercado family worked long hours to repair as many cars and trucks within the two month period before their exodus from Gilroy. Don Juan slept soundly and snored loud enough for Yiwu to hear it from outside. One morning, while Yiwu slept, Rosalinda visited his shed. She put her index finger to his lips to indicate for him to keep quiet. She slipped under the sheets with him and just embraced him without saying a single word. Fifteen minutes later she got up and left as quietly as she had entered. Rosalinda made coffee and some tortillas before the kids got up to go to school. Don Juan woke up tired and asked the kids to help with the auto repairs. Rosalinda objected to them missing school. Johnny Junior wanted to stay and help too, but Rosalinda sent him off to school with Coca.

Don Juan did not live up to his part of the agreement to not physically abuse Rosalinda. She avoided showing her face to Yiwu, out of fear of what he would do if she showed him her lower lip, swollen like she had been in a boxing match. After the second day of not seeing Rosalinda in the kitchen, he was suspicious about her absence. He could not see himself sending Rosalinda and her family away. He left the house wearing American clothing, a suit and a nice white shirt with a black tie. He returned after dark and he went right into the shed for the night.

One week later, Rosalinda made an appearance in the kitchen. Her lip healed well but the light blue bruise colored her lower jaw. She smiled at Yiwu with her face turned away. Yiwu's body tightened with anger and he clinched his fists. Killing Don Juan occupied his mind, abandonment filled his thoughts, but how could he leave Rosalinda? His love for Rosalinda was so strong that it clouded his mind; how could he leave her because he loved her? Yet he knew he had to sacrifice his love in order for her to have an opportunity to have a home for her family.

"What happened?" he asked.

"Don Juan says I don't want to make love to him any more. He's right! I don't want to kiss him anymore, either. Now that my heart belongs to Yiwu, Don Juan can no longer have my body either. I will stay with him because I love my kids, this I must do!"

"I must leave you and Don Juan in my house. You need a place to live with your family. I must leave before I kill him and go to jail," declared Yiwu with certainty.

143

"We will leave in a couple of weeks and you can have your house back." Rosalinda looked right at Yiwu's angry face. They walked back to the shed and made quiet love for thirty minutes. Each minute was a precious as extracting the sweet nectar of a passion fruit. Those thirty minutes settled the beast growling inside Yiwu's heart. *"Te amo mi amor, Yiwu,"* her lips parted to bid him farewell, *"I love you, my love,"* Rosalinda looked radiant as she floated quietly into the house.

A week later, the postman finally delivered the letter Yiwu was waiting for, a letter from Santa Clara County Records Office. He packed a shoulder bag, filled a few things in a pillowcase and waited for Rosalinda to come downstairs. When she did, he hand-delivered a sealed envelope. She took the letter from him with a puzzled look on her face. With a more present concern on hand, however, she distorted her face to signal that little Johnny was on his way downstairs. Yiwu gave Rosalinda the envelope and informed her that he had signed over the title of the house to her, Rosalinda Mercado and not to tell Don Juan. *"The title to this house is in your name. You now own this house. I will leave. Your family can now have a house to live in."* Giving Rosalinda the house for her family, a place to raise her children made Yiwu smile.

"I don't want this house if it means you won't be in it," cried Rosalinda.

"What's going on down here?" demanded Don Juan.

"Mi Chinito is leaving before he kills you for hurting me!" yelled Rosalinda. *"It is your fault he is leaving!"*

"I will kick the shit out of you, Chinaman!" threatened Don Juan, not thinking of what happened the last time he and Yiwu had an encounter.

Yiwu walked calmly outside where he waited for Juan. Juan's reasoning told him that the only reason Rosalinda was not participating in lovemaking was because she had fallen in love with the Chinaman. He attacked Yiwu, and was flipped into space, landing hard on his back. He threw fists and feet at Yiwu and again the punches and kicks were blocked and he landed on his back.

Yiwu picked up his belongings in the pillowcase and swung it around his right shoulder, turned to face Don Juan and looked at him man-to-man, *"If not for Rosalinda, you would be a dead man,"* and he walked up the street toward the bus terminal.

A year later, on the same day Yiwu left, Don Juan vanished. A missing person's report was filled, but no one had any interest in looking for him. From that day on, the kids showered, got dressed, ate breakfast, and went to school on schedule. The kids had become competent mechanics and were able to make a living out of repairing vehicles. The auto repair business went on as if Don Juan was still running it. At the end of the day, Rosalinda often wondered which man would return first, but she secretly prayed it would be Yiwu.

Chapter 12

Twelve Black Roses

In all regions of the universe, black holes exist in a space-time continuum where gravity prevents anything, including light, from escaping. This idea holds true throughout outer space where a black hole creates an event horizon that marks the point of no return. This event absorbs all the light that hits the horizon, reflecting nothing from its surface.

The color black has had different associations throughout the ages: it has represented evil sources like witches, bogeyman, and death. It has also designated powerful figures: such as judges, clergy, and law enforcement officers. The aristocracy in Europe once forbade dressing in black clothes, then reversed course and adopted dressing in black as a symbol of royalty. The color black affects the mind and body in so many powerful ways: black helps create an inconspicuous feeling, false confidence in appearance, increasing a sense of potential and possibility, including feelings of emptiness, gloom, and despair.

Black travels in a world where there is no transmission, reflection, or diffusion of its image. All sorts of demented creatures walk the empty streets, dark allies, or wait by the back door of a cantina.

Evil dresses in black and in his heart turns black. Black travels in a world where there is no transmission, reflection, or diffusion of its image. To live in that world for a few hours or days, as he knows he must, in order to carry out his mission without detection; he covers himself in black and hardens his heart so that it, too, is black. He closes his eyes, and withdraws into himself, preparing to be awakened into the ruthless monster that can kill with impunity, with no regard for humanity. He is only too aware that when he eventually awakens from this altered state; the actions of a damaged heart will have left behind a trail of dead bodies. Call it what you will, it is a form of justice.

*　　　　*　　　　*　　　　*　　　　*

Since the Twelve Roses Case, as it is officially called, law enforcement offices in the Bay Area had come under constant ridicule by the media and the general public for not making much progress with so many unsolved cases. In addition to the community feeling empathy for the farm laborers butchered by Julio Cortez, better known as El Coyote, they felt relieved that their overnight hero, the Serial Killer's Killer, popularly referred to as SKK, was out there on patrol. His popularity spread by word of mouth, throughout the San Francisco Bay Area and the neighboring counties. There was talk in the Hollywood circles that a movie on the Serial Killer's Killer would educate law enforcement on how to capture serial killers. With television programming of cops movies and a mini-series on serial killers becoming so popular, a new show about a vigilante carrying out the justice for a broken legal system would get high ratings. The local television stations confronted the police for committing so few resources to capturing the many serial killers roaming the streets. To make law enforcement look worse, every talk show seemed to be discussing and displaying pictures of unsolved homicides.

For Diego, the excitement of working at the Berkeley Police Department became somewhat diminished when Chi was transferred back to the Oakland Police Department. He was accustomed to seeing Chi when he walked by her desk. He did not look forward to attending another meeting on SKK; the clever serial killer had everyone guessing his whereabouts. So little was known about him. After the Garlic Festival, everyone looked at each other and wondered if they were staring at a serial killer among them. After numerous meetings on the SKK, the following is what they knew about him:

Serial Killer's Killer, possibly Asian

> Height 6 feet to 6'1"

> Weight 180lbs-200lbs

> Knows about forensics

> Practices martial arts

> Has access to police files

> Motive (undetermined)

The SKK files were labeled after the number of roses left at each crime scene. The files described an intelligent and meticulous character that carefully plans his crimes, constructs elaborate altars with a hodgepodge of offerings like candles, incense, tea, bread, coffee, corn, Mexican sweetbread, and religious funerary art statues. He carefully displays pictures and newspaper articles implicating the murdered victims. On the Eleven Roses Case, promotional publications practically announced that the location of the next killing would be at the Oakland Coliseum, home of the Silver and Black, and the Raider Nation. *"Ok, that's Great,"* thought Diego. *"Raiders, pirates, and a full of other deranged strangers."*

A loud banging on the front door woke up Chi and Diego on an early Sunday morning. Still in his boxers, Diego opened the door, shielding his eyes from the sun.

"Diego de Campos?" questioned an FBI agent.

"Yes, what is it?" asked Diego in a pissed-off tone.

"Get dressed, the FBI wants to ask you some questions about SKK," demanded the agent.

"This is Sunday morning for Christ's sake!" Diego protested, knowing full well that the federal government was in total control:

they owned the property where Diego lived, had remote access to open the gate, could arrest him and deliver him to the FBI at the police station.

Down at Berkeley Police Department, Captain Williams greeted Diego and the FBI agent. The captain patted Diego on the shoulder as he entered the interrogation room.

"Wait outside, Captain Williams," ordered the FBI agent.

"Wait a minute here, he's my detective. I have to be present!" demanded Williams.

"Wait outside, Captain Williams!" ordered the agent with a long stare.

The door closed and Diego remained standing, while the agent sat at opposite end of the table. Some pictures and papers were arranged in an orderly fashion front of the agent. Diego remained standing and waited for the barrage of questions. He had been at the opposite end of the interrogation thousands of times, but this time he really felt how it was to be at the receiving end. The focus of the questions immediately revealed that the agents belief that SKK was a police insider. While the Rose Case files had an abundance of evidence, not one credible piece of evidence pointed to any suspect. After an hour, the agent changed the line of questioning, *"Do you know Carlos Santos?"*

"Yes, he is my best friend since childhood," answered Diego.

"Do you know Julio Cortez?"

"No, never heard of him!"

"He is known as El Coyote!"

"If you are implying that Carlos has a connection with the Garlic Festival murder, you are mistaken. Carlos is a kind person."

"Did he know Julio Cortez, El Coyote?"

"Carlos knew of him, but he never met El Coyote."

"Do you know Angélica?"

"Has something happened to Angélica?" Diego rushed to the table and sat down and cooperated more fully with the investigation.

"Listen Detective de Campos, SKK is an intelligent criminal and he knows his forensics, he leaves sufficient evidence to implicate his victims as serial killers, then exits the scene without leaving a trace."

"You are not saying Carlos is SKK?"

"Carlos has been arrested and Angélica and the baby have been reported missing,"

"How can I help?"

"Do you know if Carlos had a motive for wanting to kill El Coyote?"

"Yes, but Carlos is not the Serial Killer's Killer!"

"Answer the question, Diego!" the agent raised his voice.

"Yes, Julio Cortez was involved in large scale human trafficking and Angélica was also smuggled across the border by El Coyote, that is his modus operandi," Diego stood up and walked around the table towards the agent.

"What else do you know about Julio Cortez and Carlos Santos?" finally the agent declared. *"Did he have a motive?"*

"Well, it does look like he had a motive for this crime, but what about the motives for all the other homicides?" To change his direction, Diego spun around on one foot with disbelief and doubt that his friend could ever kill anybody. He knew that Carlos would know how to enter and leave a crime scene without leaving evidence. Diego thought of something with such significance that it drained the blood from his face and momentarily, he turned pale. The FBI

agent noticed his facial expression but did not ask Diego about it. He knew Diego wouldn't share it with him anyhow.

The agent was authorized to use whatever method possible to capture SKK. Just then the door opened, and three large men walked in, with two of them protecting the one in the middle. The one in the middle was Carlos. Diego stood up when he recognized Carlos. Diego approached him with a big hug, *"un fuerte abrazo amigo, so good to see you, Carlos!"*

One of the guards wedged in between them and directed Carlos to keep his distance from Diego, *"No touching! Stay across the table."*

"We are old friends!" declared Diego with disappointment at the guard's behavior.

"Can you believe it, they think I might be the Serial Killer's Killer?" questioned Carlos with indignation. *"For a while, they thought you, Diego, might be SKK. Yeah! A Mexican Serial Killer's Killer, pretty damn low probability of that happening!"*

" Carlos, *they don't have a clue, so they suspect everybody. I was questioned as if I were SKK."* He sat down on the wooden chair and felt something in his back pocket. Carlos had slipped something in his pocket when they embraced. The agent noticed the discomfort on Diego's face and wondered what it might be.

"What's the matter, detective Campos?" asked the agent.

"I am getting a really bad stomachache from all this bullshit. It is improbable that Carlos is SKK. He has a newborn and a very sick mother," argued Diego.

"If you are not SKK, then who is?" the agent asked with a sarcastic tone.

"Have you read my forensics report on the 11 Roses homicide?" asked Carlos of the agent. *"SKK can find plenty of serial killers in the Bay Area and execute them, and even with the law enforcement officers*

turning over every stone, you can't find who leaves an altar full of clues so that you can catch him. You still have no idea. So what do you do, blame lab technicians and detectives," Carlos ridiculed the FBI agency and police departments.

"Well, if you are not him, and you seem to know so much, who is SKK?" asked the agent.

"You ought to be focusing on who is the SKK's next kill? Read my forensics' report, I think the answer is there," directed Carlos. *"He told us who his next kill will be and where he'll kill'em."*

Diego jumped in, *"You know, he's right! Focus on finding out who will be SKK's next victim. Let me review the report,"* he requested.

"The report is classified," responded the agent.

"Well, do you want me to help?"

"This visit is over!" the agent stood up and walked to the door and exited."

The two guards escorted Carlos back to his cell. Diego felt something in his back pocket and pulled out a wad of paper rolled into a ball. Later in back seat of the patrol car, he unrolled a note that read 24 Hour Fitness #112. He stuffed it back into his pocket, and walked to the 24 Hour Fitness on Webster Street, where Carlos had mentioned he went to work out his anxiety.

Inside the gym locker, writing on an envelope read: *"Take the money and find a safe place for Angélica and Carlitos. They are in Las Conejeras. I knew that the FBI would keep the forensics report away from you because the report suspects that you are SKK and it describes other evidence that the FBI wants to keep for their eyes only: vials and syringes which contained traces of anabolic/androgenic steroids, banned substances by the National Football League."*

*   *   *   *   *

The full moon was in the early evening sky when the Oakland Raiders in their Silver and Black burst out of the locker room and into the howling of the Raider Nation, that unruly alliance whose incomprehensible noise transmits only static over the air waves: men and women from all walks of life with black and silver painted faces, dressed as pirates, skeletons all growling at the moon. The Raider Nation inspires the Raiders to win at home; they are like no other fans in the National Football League. Regardless whether the team is winning or losing, the Raider Nation comes to let out the savage out for at least those three hours of the game. The Raider Nation does not need an enemy; they fight among each other until someone is carried out on a gurney.

Odds were always for the Oakland Raiders to win, in their slick Silver and Black, to defeat the opposing team, even one with a better win/loss record. If the opposing team played a hard physical game for the first three quarters and then tired, the Raiders could pull out a win, especially if Kenny Stabler, the Snake, was behind the ball. He didn't care how he looked out in the field as long as the Raiders won. The Raiders could be scored on early in the game, but as the banging and tackling continued through the third quarter, Kenny would then start scoring touchdown after touchdown. He looked at the opponents as if he was studying them from underneath the brim of a tilted cowboy hat. He would call a play straight at an opponent who was injured on a previous play.

Kenny Stabler, number 12, would slither away from tacklers and release an ugly pass to a receiver in time to win the game. The epitome of excellence in football lore is the game with the most unbelievable Raider touchdown against the San Diego Chargers. The Chargers were in the lead, 20-14 and there were only ten seconds remaining on the clock. The Chargers did not count on the Snake slithering again, fumbling the ball forward, rolling into the end zone nor did they anticipate that the Raider wide receiver, Casper, would pounce on it to tie the score, 24 to 24. The Raiders kicked the extra point and won the game. After this game, the

Raiders referred to the forward fumble as the Holy Roller or as the Immaculate Deception. Consequently, the NFL changed the ruling: If a player fumbles after the two-minute warning in a half, or on fourth down at any time during the game, only the fumbling player can recover and advance the ball. If that player's teammate recovers the ball during those situations, it is placed back at the spot of the fumble.

The "Just Win, Baby" culture invaded the minds and hearts of the players and the whole franchise. The message: "win at any cost." The front four on both sides of the ball were not men, but giants. Men were not supposed to be 300-400 pounds and still be able to run as fast as they do and leap ten feet in the air and catch a football. The defenses were recording more tackles and sacks, year by year. The abuse of anabolic steroids became pervasive throughout all sports, but most evident in football. The arena, the Oakland Coliseum, was no longer the place where the gladiators and the fans could leave their aggressions at the game. Aggression and violence spilled out into the streets and into the bedrooms at an alarming rate. The abuse of steroids was beginning to have an adverse effect on players and also their families.

There was a dramatic increase of domestic violence involving football players' family members. The number of deaths involving football players reached an unacceptable level; divorces of NFL football players were destroying the image of the NFL family.

The committee members assigned to review the abuse of banned substances by the NFL were disturbed upon learning the statistics on football players. Players endured the physical trauma to the body, however the worst damage of all, was the blows to the head. The addiction to winning became more intense with the use of steroids; and the desire to improve performance was magnified by the idea that winning was the only thing that mattered. On two Super Bowl games the Raiders won, the quarterback and the coach were Mexican American, but of most important fact was that many of the Raiders claimed that they had taken anabolic/androgenic steroids, the ones banned by the NFL. It had been known for many years that most of the players used steroids. The sports doctors and trainers encouraged the use of steroids. Some players claimed that 90% of the players he knew used steroids. One of them, weighed less than one hundred pounds when he died at 39 years of age, his playing weight had been 280lbs.

Captain Williams supervised one team of investigators, forensics technicians, and profilers to look for possible SKK suspects in their review of football agents, coaches, players, and owners in relationship with the abuse of anabolic/androgenic steroids. During the meeting, the team speculated that if they were successful at preventing the next execution, SKK might possibly determine that law enforcement is carrying out justice, and choose to stop the killings.

Bay Area police departments started a campaign to carry out justice by arresting prostitutes, drunks, and embezzlers, as well as doctors for malpractice and lawyers for practicing without a license. The jails, rehabilitation centers, and mental health centers were filled to capacity within a few months. The media covered law enforcement's response to the increased crime rate in the Bay Area, and Captain Williams knew that in all likelihood, SKK was learning about the effort to address all aspects of illegal activity, including serial killers. They arrested some suspects, but eventually had to let them loose since they did not have credible evidence against them.

Carlos Santos' insistence that SKK will strike someone involved with the use of banned substances in the Oakland Raider organization had yielded his release from jail. Carlos requested to join the team under Captain Williams who was investigating the Oakland Raiders for an upcoming homicide. The FBI was not too happy with Captain Williams' decision to allow Carlos Santos to work the forensics side of the investigation, but it was the Captain's call and the arrangements were made with the Oakland Police Department. Looking for an individual who is largely responsible for the abuse of banned substances was nearly impossible because so many people profited from the drug culture.

157

The FBI used computer data to link football players to sports medicine providers, and agents, which produced a list of four potential suspects. The four were brought in for questioning about their knowledge of the abuse of banned substances. The investigation team reached consensus on the two most likely suspects. The first suspect was brought in and sat on the chair next to the door. He sat down, made himself comfortable, straightened up his body and gave the interviewer a look that he was ready to be interviewed.

"What is your name and occupation?" asked the FBI agent. Other FBI agents watched the interrogation through a one-way window in the adjacent room.

"Doctor Robert E. Thompson, consultant for the Oakland Raiders."

"Do you prescribe steroids to any members of the Oakland Raiders team?"

"Yes, but not the banned substances prohibited by the NFL!"

"Do you know of any athlete under your care who has died, or been arrested in the last five years?" asked the agent looking into doctor Thompson's eyes. The doctor sat there thinking of how to answer the question, when a different question from entirely a different direction was asked, *"Do you know of any football players who are using banned substances to improve their performance?"*

Doctor Thompson was calm and answered the questions with such ease that it appeared as if he rehearsed the answers.

The second suspect entered the room with beads of perspiration on his forehead and cheeks. He seemed nervous.

"What is your name and occupation?"

"I am, I am, Dylan, Dr. Dylan Appleton, sports agent for many of the Oakland Raiders."

"Do you know which Raider football players use banned substances

to get an advantage over the other teams?" asked the FBI agent.

"Well some do, but most don't."

"Which ones use banned substances?" "Give me names, damn it!" yelled the agent pushing himself up on the table with his closed fists. *"We need your help to get to the bottom of this steroid problem."*

"I don't see a problem, the majority of the football players use steroids from the list of banned substances. There is no problem!" said Dr. Appleton. Everyone knew football has a huge problem with steroids, everyone liked it that way; big men knocking down big men and winning games was all that mattered.

"Look, Mr. Appleton, Tevita Tafokita committed suicide, three ex-Raiders have recently been arrested for violent incidents, two are in mental hospitals, and more than twenty have filed for a divorce in the last five years. My God, a Raider recently died weighing less one hundred pounds. You don't see a problem!" the agent lost his cool.

The FBI studied the four suspects to the point where they knew what kind of toilet paper they used. None of the people interviewed provided any damaging evidence. All his clients and their families respected Dr. Appleton.

The FBI released the two suspects after forty-eight hours of interrogation. The media coverage of the investigation blamed the lack of law enforcement for the rise of the Serial Killer's Killer popularity. The media called for the return of SKK, since the police departments could not make any progress on catching other serial killers in the Bay Area. The headlines read, "BRING BACK SKK!"

After two months of questioning people affiliated with football players and their performance, Carlos called Diego, *"Diego, want to go to Gilroy to visit my mother Rosa?"*

"Sure! When?" asked Diego knowing she had been ill?

"Right now! Mom is really in bad shape," answered Carlos with sadness in his voice. *"I'll pick you up within the hour."*

"OK! Can Chi come?"

"Of course, you know how we Mexicans love family."

"After all, she thinks she's Mexican!"

The lights were turned off throughout the house; lit candles of all sizes were strategically placed around Rosa's bed. Rosa slept, her frail body looked lifeless.

Her face was fleshless, the skeleton of her skull rested on the pillow. The voices of the visitors woke Rosa; she opened her eyes and recognized Diego. *"Uhhh, mijito, cuando lluegaste?"* *When did you get here? She would always ask, even if you left the room for a few minutes.*

Here she is dying and she's worrying about Carlos' friend. Diego loved Rosa, his second mother, since he spent much of his childhood at her house. Angélica came in, completely covered in black lace, hiding a sleepy baby. She had been taking care of Rosa since she was reported missing. Angélica knew that Rosa was not long for this world; she did not complain about her duties as a care provider. Diego returned to the living room and looked at the closet where he and Carlos used to hide when Rosa had customers.

"Do you want me to fix you something to eat? ¿Quieres que te haga algo que comer?" she's dying and she asks if Diego wants something to eat.

"I'll have some of your delicious tamales, Doña Rosa," Diego requested in a teasing manner. Chi punched Diego in the ribs for being disrespectful to Rosa.

"Doña Rosa está dormida," alerted Angélica as she chased everyone out of the bedroom. *"¡No está bien!"* warned Angélica. The house smelled like death had moved in and was just waiting for the soul to leave the body. Time can became rather elusive and untouchable to the mind, making life seem to be only a dream. Rosa mostly slept for another four months before lapsing into a coma and passing.

*　　　*　　　*　　　*　　　*

When Diego discussed the possibility with Chi that the SKK was Asian, she thought of it for a moment and said," *I don't think he's of Asian descent. I know everything points to SKK as being Asian, but my gut feeling tells me otherwise. Asians are private people, and SKK seeks public attention. Most of SKK's crime scenes have happened in public places; furthermore, no Asian I know would not desecrate Dzidzat.*"

"*What about the common cause of death in all of the Rose Cases, head trauma? It could be from a high martial arts kick.*"

"*Since Bruce Lee, people around the world have learned to use their feet as lethal weapons, not just Asians,*" said Chi.

"*Yeah, that's right. Ok, so what now?*"

"*We keep digging.*'

*　　　*　　　*　　　*　　　*

On early April 2012, Diego had a business meeting in San Diego and invited Chi and Carlos' family to join him at his parents' house near Governors Boulevard; where a modest house with a large garden kept Doña Ro and Don Robo busy. They grew pepinos, tomates, chile, ajo, and zanahorias in a small six by ten foot area. They looked like they were meant to be together; the two of them with the assistance of their canes took small steps in their two-hour walk around the block.

"*Roberto, wear your eye patch, you'll scare the children,*" alerted Doña Ro.

"What children? I don't see any children. I need to air out my eye socket anyway."

Little dogs would come and bark while they circled the two human statues and then they ran away barking. *"The best thing to do with dogs that have a Little Big Dog complex is to not move until they lose interest and run away,"* repeated Don Robo for the ten-thousandth time. The dogs circled another old couple that had also learned the statue trick.

Doña Ro suffered from Alzheimer's and Don Robo, with an abandoned libido, would occasionally offer flowers and candy to little girls walking by the house. It didn't take long before the neighbor's children would find an alternative route to their destination.

"Doña Ro! ¡Qué gusto de verte! What a pleasure it is to see you," Chi said as she hugged Rosario. She turned and addressed Don Robo, *"¡Hóla, Don Robo!"*

"¡Hola!" acknowledged Roberto, finally covering his eyeless socket.

Diego went about the room hugging everyone. He was home with his parents on a real vacation. For some isolated moments, he did not think about work. Diego invited everyone to dine at the Old Mexican Café in Old Town. The place was crowded, as usual; it was early afternoon on a sunny weekend day in April.

A handsome man sat alone in the corner table with three empty chairs. Diego recognized the man as Tevita Tafokitau, a Raiders' football player. He was sitting there with his head down, as he stared into his beer. As people left the restaurant, they noticed him and greeted him with admiration. *"Tevita!"* They knew him by his first name at the Old Mexican Café. Diego was star-struck. Tafokitau was one of his heroes; he did not have the nerve to greet him. Tafokitau would look over at Diego and smile as if he recognized him. The de Campos' family and friends took up a whole section of the restaurant. While the family festivities continued, Tafokitau kept smiling at the de Campos' table. The two people that he was apparently waiting for, arrived. They sat down to drink beer, eat carnitas, and greeted fans that recognized them as being Oakland Raiders. As the Tafokitau party was about to leave the restaurant, Tevita and friends walked over to the de Campos table and stopped in front of Diego.

"Hey, excuse me for staring, but aren't you Diego de Campos from the Berkeley Bears?" asked Tafokitau with a big smile.

"Yeah, how do you know me?"

"You are one of my heroes!" exclaimed Tafokitau smiling with a full mouth of white teeth. "I followed wrestling in college and saw you win every match you wrestled. I loved the way you always found a way to win especially when you were behind in points. You are a real champion!"

"You, You're my hero too! I have been following you for 13 years," said Diego with admiration.

"Uhh! Thank you, but I am retired now. Find another hero to worship!" exclaimed Tafokitau, "there are many great young players now. "Take care!"

*   *   *   *   *

The interviews with some of Doctor Appleton's associates gave a different picture of the type of character he was than the one who was interviewed earlier. One person described how Doctor Appleton manipulated the NFL draft. Appleton was more manipulative with the ready-to- retire football players than the rookies. He supplied anabolic/androgenic steriods to football players who should retire, just to make a little more money on them. Doctor Appleton's bank accounts and tax records would be evidence in the exposure of the level of corruption that was rampant throughout the National Football League.

Doctor Appleton was brought into the Oakland Police Department for further questioning. He appeared collected and more confident than before. He asked for a glass of water as he waited for the interrogation to begin. Doctor Appleton drank a sip of water and sat there looking overconfident. Diego made him wait, while other detectives studied him. Diego had a hunch about the doctor; he was too cool to be human. Perhaps Dr. Appleton was living in a completely compartmentalized closet in his mind and as a result, he was incapable of recognizing his real self. The doctor had become "Doctor Appleton." In this state of mind, the police cannot detect the evil side of someone's nature, not even on a lie detector test. Up against Diego's gut feeling, they did not have any credible evidence to detain the doctor. Diego was not the only detective who was completely fed up with the legal restrictions prohibiting law enforcement from detaining a suspect without sufficient credible evidence. Time and time again, he saw law enforcement let a suspect go, and it made him sick to his stomach when evil men used that opportunity to kill again. There's a part of me, he acknowledged, who would really like to stop waiting for everything to neatly fall into place and just take the law into my own hands and put these guilty son of a bitches in their graves. Countless times, law enforcement has had a suspect in their custody, only to let them go to kill again.

At a meeting to rehash the Rose Case Files, Carlos asked about the color of the roses found at each of the Rose Cases. As they rummaged through the pictures and files specifically mentioning the color of the roses, the team identified that the Claremont homicide had ten red roses and eleven garlic cloves, the Gilroy festivals had pink roses and other rose cases had an assortment of colors, but not once were they black roses. And now with the connection to the Oakland Raiders and their colors Silver and Black Diego concluded, *"The Twelve Roses Case will have black roses."* Captain Williams also agreed this line of thinking had merit.

"I don't think so," Chi challenged their line of thinking. "Black roses only grow in Turkey and in some cases, nurseries can turn roses black with a black dye," added Chi with authority on Roses. Black roses are a rarity and very hard to find in the Flower District

or in the black market.

"Ok, so we have a serial killer that loves roses." Diego walked over to the counter and served himself a glass of water. "Every color had a specific meaning that SKK conveyed.

Bay Area police departments continued cleansing the streets of criminals. They were arresting many people for a variety of crimes, but just as fast as they apprehended them, they were releasing them out the back door. This was the only way to deal with the matter of arresting and incarcerating suspects at this rate; the city could not afford to keep them in jail for long.

The gladiatorial nature of football requires players to do whatever is necessary to compete in the arena, because there is no life outside the arena. The pleasure of smashing somebody down to the ground is not attainable after retirement; it may not come from the part of the brain where reasoning occurs. An impulsive strike with the back of the hand from a 275 pound fullback can knock someone out or kill them."

On May of 2010, Tevita Tafokitau, one of football's most inspirational players, committed suicide. He was just 39. He shot himself in the mouth. Apparently he could not fill the void that football created, that high profile life where he lived as the hero of the game.

After retirement, to keep himself physically fit and still able to pound his opponents into submission, the superstar was keeping fit at a neighborhood health club. His gambling, drinking, and nightlife masked what pained him more than anything; his glory had come to an end. Even off the field, Tafokitau was so loved by his fans and family. He gave his life to football, and then football took it away.

Five months later, Al Davis, the owner of the Oakland Raiders, died. He was not beloved by his players and coaches in the same way they loved Tevita Tafokitau, but he was respected and honored. He was the man most often credited for coining the phrase, *"Just win, Baby!"*

The Raiders without Al Davis were really different, *"Just win"* was not happening on the field. The Raiders were in the doldrums, with a string of losing seasons. Unfortunately, 2012 wasn't the year they would turn that around. The Raiders seemed to have lost their zeal, and the Silver and Black mystique. Through this all, the Raider organization failed to see the level of importance that the number twelve has in football. The number 12 jersey was issued to a non-quarterback player. The number 12 jersey should have been retired after Kenny Stabler, or at least not reissued, like the Dallas Cowboys and the Pittsburg Steelers had done. The number 12 jersey has been worn by some of the most famous quarterbacks: John Brodie, Joe Namath, Roger Stauback, and Terry Bradshaw. The number 12 has a symbolic reference to football teams, but especially to the Raider Nation: the twelfth player in the game symbolizes the fans; because of the support they give to the 11 players on the field. The Raiders were no longer paying attention to the symbolic significance of the color black, the number 12, and the value of the Raider Nation. The Oakland Coliseum searched the Raider Nation type spectators for weapons.

On December 16, 2012, Carlos and Diego drove to Oakland to see a Raiders' game against the Chiefs. The Oakland Raider defense dominated the game: Richard Seymour had one of his best games ever, being in the middle of each defensive play of the game. Although the Raiders won the uneventful game 15-0 with field goals, the Raider Nation was as loud and crazy as ever. With the exception of Seymour, both sides of the ball game played like renegades from a geriatrics ward.

The next morning, Diego was dispatched to the Oakland Coliseum. In the Raiders' locker room, the police found Dr. Appleton dead in his white doctor's jacket and tied to a chair. The players' lockers surrounding him were open and they contained lit candles. Incense filled the air with its scent. Some of the lockers had flowers, others had funerary offerings, and the ones with candles had publications with personal belongings related to each of the twelve rose cases. The floor around Dr. Appleton was cluttered with additional pictures, newspaper articles, and personal items from the known Rose Cases and previous cases.

Four forensics technicians from the San Francisco Police Department were cataloging the evidence. Carlos had already been there twenty minutes when Diego arrived. Diego walked around and surveyed the evidence, including the victim, when he suddenly stopped and asked aloud, *"Where is the evidence pointing to? Where? Carlos, you can figure it out, look again at the brochures and promotion publications identifying the next SKK homicide. Find me the evidence, what does it say?"*

Carlos and the technicians were logging the evidence and bagging evidence, *"We have been ordered to bag and log the evidence,"* answered a technician without looking at Diego.

"Stop! Everybody step away from the crime scene," ordered Diego. He again surveyed the crime scene for clues that would identify the location of the next SKK homicide. Since the Claremont homicide, Diego was able to find evidence which pointed to the next homicide, but nothing this time." He studied the Tarot cards and the cards with the number twelve written in different languages.

The number 12 written in different languages:

Δ‖	Attic Greek
‖∧	Egyptian
✝=	Chinese and Japanese
XII	Roman and Etruscan
‖X	Chuvash
⠒̲	Mayan

Chapter 13

Illuminate the Heavens

"Earth is the place of the fleeting
moment..." Nahuatl: Cantares Mexicanos

The fossil evidence of roses has been carbon-dated to be 35 million years old. It is believed that China introduced the cultivation of roses to Europe, some five thousand years ago. Persia probably originated the production of rose perfumes; rose oils were then made from crushing and steaming rose petals. The genus Rosa has 150 species spread throughout the Northern Hemisphere, México, and northern Africa. The popularity of the rose surged not only because of the fragrance of its perfume, or its medicinal purposes, but because the types and colors came to have symbolic value. In fifteenth century Europe, the color could have serious consequences like the War of the Roses that pitted the white rose of York against the red rose of Lancaster.

Roses have united lovers, sealed friendships, and given appreciation to special people in the world for five thousand years. The red rose has in all cultures represented passion, love, and lust, while yellow roses express appreciation and platonic love. The meaning behind the number of roses in a gift is also important; a single rose represents "I love you! Two is a marriage proposal: "Will you marry me?" Thirteen roses indicate that the recipient has a secret admirer."

*   *   *   *   *

Due to years of neglect, the gardens behind Rosalinda's house had muted roses and dried-up vegetable beds. Roses need attention and care to blossom with the fullness of their splendor. Two years went by without any rosebud blooming; insects and diseases invaded the rose and vegetable gardens. Rosalinda was not able to raise children, clean, cook, and still maintain the gardens.

One day, Rosalinda discovered that the rose and vegetable gardens were looking much better. She wondered, since none of the children had shown any inclination for farming or yard-work, *who's tending the garden*? Each rose in the garden looked healthy and they were in all stages of blooming. The yellow roses were in bloom and the pink rose bush had about ten tightly wrapped rosebuds, showing red color in their tips. Rosalinda thought of Yiwu and the beautiful gardens that he cultivated. She asked Johnny Junior, who was still living with her, if he had tended the gardens. Junior skipped dinner, he feared that Rosalinda would ask him point-blank for the identity of the mystery gardener, he would have to reveal the secret.

One night, the moon was almost full, it shone brightly in the dark starry night. Rosalinda had seen the moon in the same location through the same window and remembered it was about as full when Yiwu left town. The moonlight coming through the window made her face look powdery white. She loved that man more than her life, and now that her children were grown and could fend for themselves, she could go to him. Yiwu had loved her like no other man had. That night Rosalinda dreamed of being with him in the rose garden.

A rose may be a dark deep purple rosebud, but when it opens, it opens into a translucent lavender rose. Another rosebud may show red at its tips, yet it opens its petals to orange hues, and changes color when sunlight shines through them. When rosebuds start to open from its tightly wrapped petals, the dioxazine purple or manganese violet appears black, however at a closer study, the purple highlights on the rose, bloom from a magenta to a bright pink.

"Rosalinda, Rosalinda, come quick!" Johnny called from the rose-garden.

Rosalinda grabbed her robe, threw it around her shoulders and ran to the back of the house. "What is going on?" she asked in wonder.

"All the rose bushes are blooming, look at the red, orange, yellow, pink, coral, and white roses," declared Johnny. The rose garden looked like the floating flower gardens of Xochimilco.

"Oh, yes, they are," Rosalinda started crying.

Like all of God's creations, the gardens needed the tender loving care that can increase productivity beyond belief. The aroma of the roses floated in the air and its blend produced a rich sweet aroma. Rosalinda was so absorbed with the beauty of the moment that she did not hear or feel a person move close behind her. Rosalinda felt goose bumps throughout her neck and face, when her sense of smell informed her that Yiwu was in her presence. She turned and threw her arms around his shoulders, kissing him repeatedly. Yiwu, a very private man and a man of few words kept his love for Rosalinda to himself. He demonstrated his love for her through his actions, giving her a house for her family.

"Rosalinda, I asked Don Robo to help prepare the garden for my arrival. I asked him about your husband, Juan and he tells me, he disappeared after I left."

"Yes, he left me too. Why did you leave?" They both embraced tightly and gently kissed.

"I had to suffer alone for destroying a family and loving a married woman. I felt I had shamed you and your family. I left as a form of penance for my sins. The important thing now, is that I am back! Do you still want me to stay?"

"Of course, I will always love you, Mi Chinito."

*　　　*　　　*　　　*　　　*

The entire Oakland Coliseum was closed to the public for 48 hours after the murder at the Coliseum homicide. The coliseum was surrounded with black vehicles: vans, sedans, and motorcycles. Forensic lab technicians scrapped, swiped, and q-tipped the entire locker room, showers, and bathrooms of the Raiders and the opponents' locker rooms as well. The FBI studied all the surveillance video, interviewed security guards, and players. Nothing of interest surfaced concerning Dr. Appleton's homicide, other than he had been responsible for issuing steroids to many of the Raiders, as well as players from other teams. It finally surfaced that Dr. Appleton and other sports medicine professionals like him had been actively promoting the use of steroids by football players, and the problem became an NFL epidemic. Everyone was responsible: coaches, agents, and the players themselves, as well as the general public who paid the price of admission to see a football helmet coming off a running back's head after he had been creamed by three tacklers.

To Diego, the amount of evidence was insurmountable, what became most significant was the lack of evidence that identified the next homicide. Leaving clues to the next kill was part of the Serial Killer's Killer signature. What could that mean? Was the Twelfth Roses Case to be the last kill for SKK? Perhaps, as the working theory went if the police departments did their jobs, SKK would not have to administer his own justice.

Diego and Carlos looked into the contents of a locker labeled 4-5 Roses. It contained: a picture of a nude white male lying on the back of a nude Hispanic male; their driver's licenses were also in the locker; along with Mercury News clippings of their lives and alleged criminal activity in human trafficking, prostitution, and assaults. According to the file, the White male was a farmer who had been accused of assaulting homosexuals and raping his male workers. The Hispanic male was a labor contractor who arranged with the farmer to separate the farm labor couples by busing the males to work in Santa Cruz County, allowing the contractor to take advantage of the women left in his care. The two worked well together, feasting on their defenseless prey to fill their sexual appetites at will. The male farm workers, who were given liquor, drugs, money, and then sexually assaulted, were too embarrassed to report their assailant and the women were to afraid to report the rapes to their husbands for fear of being abandoned. In the late 1980's, the number of suicides and homicides among the migrant farmworkers was climbing to such a rate that they warranted the attention of the FBI. The FBI carried out a perfunctory investigation: interviewing just a handful of migrant workers without arresting anyone for any crime. Diego shook his head in disgust, "These damn farmers, Carlos, they always act like they own everything and everyone!"

Diego searched his memory and it occurred to him that the other phenomenon.
There was a high correlation between high school age children of the farmers who were transferred to Catholic private schools, and the high school age children of migrant families who were forcibly escorted out of Santa Clara County. Since time immemorial, young love has respected no economic or ethnic boundaries, and that was equally true for the children of farmers and the children of farm-workers, who all went to Gilroy High School, attended the same sports events and the same dances.

"When hormones are involved, kids will be kids," Diego said, "but in Gilroy, there always were some additional consequences."

Diego and Carlos remembered from their high school years that the solution was simple: the farmers terminated the employ-ment of these families, forcing them to move out of town and join the stewardship of another labor contractor. Just to make doubly sure, they almost always deposited their kids in private schools.

"Where were the bodies of 4-5 Roses found?" asked Carlos as he reviewed forensic data on the case.

"Off Hecker Pass on the way to Watsonville from Gilroy, on a bench at Mt Madonna Park!" answered Diego.

Carlos added, "Hey, these stories are real Popocatepetl love stories. You know, the story of the two lovers from different tribes who could not be together in this life, and turned themselves into volcanoes: one towering over the smaller one, as he holds her in his arms?"

"You're a romantico, Carlos!"

"If this is SKK's fourth and fifth kill, how old must he be by now?" asked Diego rubbing his right temple with his fingers.

Diego's face wrinkled as if to pose a question. "Assuming that SKK is the same person, and he is evolving into a more sophisticated serial killer, and each homicide is 3 to 4 years apart, that would be 36-48 years of killing, and let's say he was twenty years of age when he killed his first victim, that would make him 50-60 years of age."

"Carlos, you're a real Dick!" Diego said laughing loudly. "Jeez. That means we're looking for an old man, maybe someone ready to give it up?"

The altar, which was found surrounding the bench at Mt. Madonna Park did not include as many offerings as the ones found in the recent Rose Cases, nor was anything at scene of significant value, unlike the later cases.

Locker labeled **3 Roses** did not have much to review; a newspaper article on the death of one of Castroville's wealthiest farmers, Jonathan Orfanelli, known at the time as Mr. Artichoke. Three daughters survive him: Dorothy, Rebecca, Ella and ten grandchildren. He had suffered head trauma from a fall off the roof of his house. He had climbed up to remove leaves from the gutters; and slipped off the ladder; fracturing his left temple, which resulted in his death.

A tattered and discolored legal document found at the scene indicated that a Morales family had once filed legal action against Jonathan Orfanelli for fraudulently stealing their property. Due to the death of Mrs. Morales' mother, the Morales family had fallen behind their mortgage payments and taxes. They went back to México to settle their family's estate and to file for an immigration visa for Mr. Morales' mother, Mrs. Emalia Morales. They waited for the immigrations papers to be processed before returning to Castroville. The Morales' family had been late with their mortgage payments before and they were able to catch up with their payments within a few months. This time, Mr. Orfanelli used intimidation to force the bank to turn over the title to the property, especially after paying the overdue taxes and paying for the property in cash. When the Morales family returned, their belongings were in a U-Haul storage unit in town. They had no place to live so they moved into a one-room cabin in a labor camp facility.

Mr. Orfanelli had other controversies and mysteries going on in his life. His wife and wife's close male friend had been found shot to death in a hotel room in Santa Cruz. The double homicide was eventually ruled a double suicide. Diego's research found that the judge involved with the ruling of a double suicide was related to the Orfanelli family.

The last five years of Mr. Orfanelli's life were dreadful. At the encouragement of one of his daughter Ella, his teenage grandson lived with him during the summer months at his Watsonville property. One day after Mr. Orfanelli's dog, Carnicero killed the other dog in a high price dogfight, it was reported missing. Carnicero had killed the other dog right away, and then took his time in biting off the dog's flesh and eating it. Everyone who witnessed the dogfight watched in horror, the carnage by a mad dog. Carnicero was booed, but he did take home over ten thousand dollars in winnings. On dogfight nights, Carniceo was not hungry; he just drank water until he fell asleep.

Mr. Jonathan Orfanelli blamed everyone for Carnicero's disappearance. He became a bitter old man. He was vulgar with everyone he interacted with; at the grocery store: gas station, bank, and post office. To avoid him altogether, some people took an early lunch when they saw him walk into their business. When Jonathan fell off the roof, he was pronounced dead and buried with only his grandson showing up for the funeral services and at the burial site. The police did not find it odd that Mr. Orfanelli fell to his death holding the title of the Morales' property. Although he had paid the mortgage balance and taxes due, he was unable to transfer the title of the Morales' property over to his name. The property was eventually handed back to the Morales' family.

The locker labeled **2 Roses** contained two pictures of Frankie Larson, a large 13-year-old boy, who was a known bully at his Junior high school and a collection of his victims' personal belongings: jars filled with money, candy, baseballs, baseball gloves, toy trucks and cars, along with an assortment of inexpensive jewelry. His school records described him as a troubled boy who was disciplined frequently for his violations of school rules, including assaulting teachers. The school had reported Frankie to child protective service too many times and nothing was ever done. Angry parents blamed the school principal for the bruises their children hid from school officials. In an incident reported in the newspaper, the principal called 911 as a result of a boy sustaining two broken ribs from being involved in a fight with Frankie. Frankie's father, Officer Larson from the Hollister Police Department arrived at the same time as the ambulance. On the very next day, Frankie showed up to school as if nothing had happened. Frankie was detained in the principal's office and was immediately sent home on a week's suspension. By third day of the suspension, angry parents demanded that Frankie Larson be expelled from the school. The school district called for a special hearing on the expulsion of Frankie Larson. The boardroom was crowded with angry parents whose children had been bullied by Frankie. About half of the boys at school were at one time or another physically assaulted by Frankie. Except for Officer Larson, no one came to Frankie's defense. The proceeding was so unruly and heated at times that the board called for a continuance to the next special board meeting, meanwhile, Frankie would remain suspended.

Frankie's aggressive nature was present since childhood. He was born pre-mature and was sickly for the first six months of his life; Frankie was an unhappy infant and that never changed. Officer Larson wishing to have a son to relive the best part of his life, playing sports in high school and college was sadly disappointed by Frankie's lack of interest in sports. Most disheartening was that Frankie was not athletic.

The sport he did enjoy was running into people and knocking

boys down to the ground. Since he was six inches taller and weighed fifty pounds more than anyone else at school, he pushed his weight around. After enduring much abuse, his classmates started calling him, "Frankie-Stein", which infuriated Frankie. Some of his classmates would readily give away their money, candy, or anything else he wanted just to make him leave them alone.. The boys at school did not put up a fight against him. "Here Frankie, my lunch and two dollar bills," they said before he would ask for anything else. He was like a bull without a corral; he didn't know his boundaries. He even harassed the principal.

At an exhibition baseball game, between two Junior high schools, Frankie took away the baseball mitt and ball from a little boy. The little boy cried, but no one stopped Frankie from walking away with his new possessions. Another little boy sitting on the bleachers stood up and swiftly took the baseball glove away from Frankie's hand, Frankie could not believe that someone would dare take things away from him. Without mentioning the names of the students involved in the altercation, the newspaper article described the incident as a bullying attack. The article did mention information from the medical records of the incident: student sustains stitches on the lower lip and left eye. The incident was reported and once again Frankie received a two-week suspension. He liked his little vacations from school.

Two days before the expulsion hearing, Frankie Larson was reported missing by his father.

Frankie Larson had been riding his bike to school, because he was denied bus service due to his many altercations with his classmates. Two blocks from school, tall bushes lined the sidewalk; the students walked by the overgrown bushes to the stoplight. Twenty minutes before the end of the school day, Frankie rode his bike to the bushes and hid with his bike. Out of nowhere, Frankie found himself being punched on the face. Frankie's leg was pinned under the frame of the bike and the handlebars stuck him in the ribs knocking the air out of his lungs. The bat that Frankie had taken from a fifth grader was used to strike him on the forehead.

178

His body went limp and remained pinned under his bike. Late in the afternoon, a bike belonging to Frankie was found near the school grounds. Officer Larson picked up the bike and drove slowly past the bushes. He noticed that two rose bushes had been planted within the bushes. By mid-May, bright orange roses densely crowned the two rose bushes. The people that couldn't help themselves from snipping a rose: always snipped two.

The locker labeled **Rose**, had articles and stories of dogs bred for fighting. One of the pictures was of a Mr. Orfanelli's black and gold Doberman pincher, Carnicero. He was a large dog with large fangs taking up most of the picture. In the locker was a missing dog report offering a thousand dollar reward of the return of the dog to Mr. Orfanelli.

Carlos had a friend living in Castroville who knew the Orfanelli's and about Carnicero. James Peace had been a Gilroy police officer until he shattered his left leg and had broken four ribs in an automobile accident. James was retired on disability, but he still wanted to work as a security guard at the shipyard in Monterey. He was nearly bald and had just turned sixty. He joined Diego and Carlos at a pub on Monterey harbor. He limped up to the bar and looked around for his friends. Carlos and Diego were deep in conversation at a booth when James limped up and sat down.

"Carlos, hey Diego, been taking down any dolls lately," James acknowledged Diego's reputation as a wrestler and a ladies man.

"Look, here!" Diego showed off his wedding ring." We had a quiet wedding at city hall, since she did not have parents to give her away."

"Never thought you were the marrying type!"

"You should take a look at his wife's picture at the New Years' party," teased Carlos.

Diego turned serious, "James, we asked you to meet with us to discuss some homicides. Starting with the double homicide of the labor contractor and the farmer found nude in Mt. Madonna, followed by the deaths of Mr. Orfanelli and Frankie Larson."

"Fellas, that's a lot of meat and potatoes. Well, about the double homicide, there were rumors that the farmer took one farm worker over to work in Santa Cruz from a Gilroy farm and on the way, he stopped at Mt. Madonna, got him drunk and then sodomized him while he was passed out. Rumor was he did that a lot. None of them he raped filed a police report. In terms of Orfanelli, the word was that he was asking to be knifed by one of those Mexican farm workers that he thinks he owns. I have my suspicions that if he fell off the roof, it was probably more like pushed off the roof by someone with a grudge."

"How did you find this information out?" asked Carlos.

"I still like chasing skirts and I have been lucky that I can almost always find some willing señorita to go for a quick spin with this bald old man," said James with a wide smile on his face.

"How would they know such confidential information about their customers?" asked Diego.

"When men drink, they spill their guts, even if it offends God!"

"Done that, wore the shirt. I have been told that when I drink, I tell my friends as I hug and kiss them, "I love you, man!""

"What about Orfanelli? Do *you* think he fell off the roof?" asked Diego finishing his second Corona beer.

"Yeah, he fell off the roof, but he had help, if you know what I mean. Orfanelli was a son of a bitch, but he was healthy and strong. He could beat the shit out of any one of us. He was so mean that his family disowned him. He was not invited to their Christmas or birthday parties."

"Why?" asked Carlos not understanding the extent of the

banishment?

"Orfanelli was not born rich, he stole, cheated, and some say he killed his competitors to become one of the richest businessmen in California."

"James, I can see his business partners not liking him, but his family?" asked Diego as James now had his full attention.

"His family believed he killed his wife."

"I read that too, and I could see why the wife's family would not like him, but his own family shunned him too." as a Mexican caring for his mother, Carlos found this behavior to be incomprehensible.

"Who was with him when Orfanelli fell off the roof?" asked Diego.

"Orfanelli was self-reliant, he must have climbed up the ladder by himself as he often did. His teenage grandson who was living with him during the summer months found him when he returned from a grocery store run."

Carlos' phone rang as he drank the last gulp of his third Corona. His face immediately wrinkled with sadness. "Got to go! My mother, Rosa has turned for the worse. I think this is it, she is passing tonight."

Carlos and Diego drove in separate cars to Rosa's Cantina. A crowd had gathered in Rosa's room. Rosa was still breathing, but everyone knew that her time had come. Carlos held her hand while he listened to her breathing.

"Carlitos, where is Juan Carlos!" asked Rosa weakly.

"He is sleeping," said Carlos softly. He waived at Diego, "wake Juan Carlos!"

"Carlitos!

"Aquí estoy, Rosa, mi corazón!

"I see the bright light, the light is calling me" Rosa's eyes opened and widened a little. "Dios mio, ay voy." The light came from within the dilated pupils. The look was not one of the lights going out of the eyes, but one of light becoming brighter. Rosa Santos' soul bloomed like a white rose and light emanated from her into a universe infinitely full of stars.

On December 21, 2012, the day declared to be the end of the world according to interpretations of the Mayan Calendar, Rosa Santos passed at 11:11pm. That night, Carlos and Diego slept next to Rosa on some pad called a mattress.

Farm workers are early risers; not one of the farm workers was caught sleeping by the time the sunrise peaked over the Gabilan Mountains. James showed up at 7:00am to offer his condolences to Carlos. Diego helped find a glass vase for the dozen red roses that James brought for Rosa. Everybody knew that Rosa liked red roses. James and Diego walked outside with the pozole that Cristina brought over at 5:30am.

"James, I am sorry that I have to be so insensitive of Carlos' loss, but we are also here on an investigation and we did not get to finish our interview."

"No, no, no, Diego! A detective's work is never done," teased James.

"Want another bowl of pozole?"

"Does my dick wake up when Junior sees a pretty señorita?"

"Still a horny toad! Ah James?"

James drove Diego over to where Frankie's bike was found. The bushes had not been watered and they looked bone dry. Diego spotted the rose bushes and asked, "When were these bushes planted?"

"They appeared after Frankie went missing."

"Have you seen this small cross between the two rose bushes?"

"It's the first time I've seen it," answered James.

"His body was never found, right?"

"Right."

Diego looked at the rose bushes and a thought came to him, *Frankie is buried under the rose bushes*. Diego called the Hollister Police Department to come and investigate the possibility of discovering Frankie Larson's burial site. The police came and they called their chief to acquire permission to dig, within ten minutes, a forensics team arrived and assisted with unearthing Frankie's body.

"James, tell me where did Mr. Orfanelli live?" asked Diego.

"Not far from here, get in the car and I'll drive you there."

"What are you looking for?" asked James.

"A rose bush!" answered Diego with excitement in his voice.

At Orfanelli's house, they walked the property looking for a single rose bush. James found an unkempt bush that had not been pruned in years. A single yellow rose blossom stared at Diego from a distance. *I am here*, the rose spoke to him. A dog collar dangled from one of the center branches. The forensic team had followed James to Orfanelli's house. They brought their tools and set them down next to the pecan tree. The technicians worked slowly, Diego and James were excited that they might be solving another murder within a one-hour period. The bones of the large dog were intact. The forensic technicians stated that it was definitely a dog and it had a fractured skull.

The Hollister Police gave a news conference early Monday morning: The police chief and mayor of Hollister together made the announcement, "The afternoon of August 13, 1980, Detective de Campos from the Berkeley Police Department working on a lead to a series of murders over the last thirty to forty years, found the skeletal remains of a young boy and those of a canine. Detective de Campos believes that these deaths are connected and maybe tied to an on-going investigation of a serial killer who has been terrorizing the San Francisco Bay Area and surrounding counties."

Unfortunately, instead of focusing on the potential break in the investigation, the local and national television stations sensationalized the series of crimes as their lead story for three consecutive days; *The Serial Killer's Killer also known to law enforcement as SKK, guards the streets throughout the Bay Area while the police departments apparently sleep. They might as well sleep, since the list of serial killers in the Bay Area continues to grow every year. SKK administers justice, and is apparently the Bay Area's guardian of society's castaways, those who lack a voice."*

*   *   *   *   *

Father Ignacio and Mother Superior waited for Doña Ro's visit with anticipation. Members of the Italian community protested opening the doors of the Catholic Church to the likes of Rosa Santos. Some influential men who in their youth had visited Rosa also protested. They didn't protest because they disliked her or were unsatisfied customers; they felt they had to because they enjoyed the benefits that accrued from their positions of authority as elected officials and they knew their supporters would demand it. In fact, they ended up liking and respecting Rosa Santos more than the women in their lives. Rosa was a real person, funny, and very bright. None of her visitors ever complained about the $500 they paid for their visit with her.

Rosario used her cane to walk, her spine no longer kept her

upright. Her back curved forward at the shoulders, forcing her to always look down. Don Robo with a black patch over his eye, opened the door and Rosario walked into Father Ignacio's office.

"Doña de Campos, mucho gusto en verla, good to see you," Father Ignacio took Rosario's hand and kissed the back of it.

"Vengo con un corazón herido, I come to see you with a broken heart," said Rosario looking right into his eyes under the grey bushy eyebrows. Don Robo, standing behind her, trembled, that the church may tumble into rubble if they will not allow Rosa to have a mass and proper farewell. Mother Superior was tight lipped and determined to stay out of the conversation; she was a mere witness and there simply to provide spiritual support to Father Ignacio.

"Please come to our seating area," invited Father Ignacio.

"No, thank you. We won't be staying long. This is not a social visit, Father. We are many here, and we demand that the church open its doors to Rosa Santos and send her to God with a proper farewell."

"Our church members have concerns with having a wake for Rosa Santos..." began Father Ignacio while inching closer to Mother Superior.

Don Robo in work clothes looked like a suspicious character, especially with a black patch over his eye. He stood behind Doña Ro as she addressed Father Ignacio. "Rosa Santos has done more good for this community than you will ever be able to do in your lifetime. So, listen carefully."

Doña Ro moved a few steps closer to Father Ignacio, Don Robo stepped up to stand next to Rosario, and he took his eye patch off, put it in his pocket, exposing an empty eye socket. Don Robo forgave Rosa for the loss of his eye. He thanked her for therapy lessons that made him a kinder person.

"Rosa Santos desfrutó la vida, dia por dia: she enjoyed life every single day, regretting not going on to college, but not giving life to Carlitos, her son to love for the rest of her life," confirmed Rosario.

"Yes, we know that she was a happy person and many men loved her," said Father Ignacio thinking of the many confessions that he had heard over the years.

"Father Ignacio, you have known me since you came to Gilroy twenty years ago, and in all our meetings you have paid me respect and you have been a most gracious spiritual leader. Father, you will make all the necessary arrangements to assist in preparing a memorable farewell for Rosa Santos."

"I can not....."

"You can, and you will honor Rosa Santos on the day her family chooses. Father Ignacio, if Rosa Santos is not welcomed in this church, neither am I, nor any of the Mexicans living in Gilroy, Hollister, and Morgan Hill will ever step foot into this church again."

Doña Ro turned and walked towards the door. Don Robo put his eye patch back on and addressed both Father Ignacio and Mother Superior, "I have been thinking about publishing a list of scholarship sponsors who each donated $500 to the college education fund for Carlitos Santos!"

*   *   *

In early morning light, Yiwu took Rosalinda for a drive to Christmas Hill Park. It had been raining when he parked the ford truck next to a large oak tree. Two large granite boulders protected the tree trunk. On the base of the boulder on the north side of the tree was a smaller boulder with four letters carved into it, "Popo." Rosalinda looked at Yiwu with sadness in her eyes for the loss of

186

her son, and happy that Yiwu had memorialized the life that had lived in her. "Thank you Yiwu!" said Rosalinda kissing the palm of his hand. Yiwu brought a small Chinese funerary urn, placed it on Popo's rock, filled it with family papers and lit it. Rosalinda and Yiwu prayed in their own way. Rosalinda loved the way Yiwu had prepared her for this celebration of her stillborn son.

He pointed to some trees nearby. "See the two trees over there? Rosalinda could see where an oak tree had fallen between the two main branches of another oak tree and with time, the two trees grew into each other." The fallen tree had stayed alive only by the nourishment that it obtained from the oak tree that was still rooted to the ground. "Without your love, I cannot live any more," Yiwu said holding tightly onto Rosalinda.

"I cannot live without your love, either, Yiwu," Rosalinda kissed his neck. "The only thing that gave me a reason to live during our long separation was our little boy, Jimmy, " she said. "Every time I looked at him, I saw you. He was the best reminder of our love and he showed me that happiness for me was possible. You are the one who gave me the courage to stand on my own two feet."

After an hour at the park, he drove Rosa to the Catholic Church on First and Monterey Street.

Rosa Santos's coffin was taken out of a black Hertz and lifted by six men in white long-sleeved guayaberas with affoza pleats and Western-style yokes. The light rain slowed down to a drizzle before the sun came out. The granite steps, the church walls, and the people's spirit all looked freshly cleansed. The cars that turned the corner on First and Monterey Street honked their horns. On the steps to the church entrance, handsome men dressed in black suits stopped the procession and one at a time took their place as pallbearers. Rosa's customers had come to thank her in this special way for helping them when they needed to realign their world.

The organ music was loud but not intrusive and the boys' choir sang softly as if to help slowly move the coffin forward. Four little girls dressed in communion-white dresses handed out white rose hair-clips for the women and for the men, white rose lapel pins. The church was full of people from throughout the bay area and relatives from México. Representatives from the mayor's office were in attendance as they inched their way forward to visit with Rosa. The chief of police walked in with three officers marching behind him. The cantina owners and many of their customers were a dominant presence. The voices floated up the church steeples in a Coriolis effect within the domes. In Latin, Father Ignacio welcomed everyone to a mass honoring Rosa Santos. "The gates of heaven have opened up today for your child, Holy Father." The coffin stopped momentarily in front of him and he blessed it, "En el nombre del padre, del hijo, e Espiritú Santo!" The pallbearers placed the coffin on a marble table and opened the casket.

Inside the coffin, Rosa Santos' body rested on a bed of white rose petals. Her face looked younger than seventy-eight years of age, her lips parted slightly as if hiding a secret with a smile. Although her eyes were closed, the eyelids seemed to be slightly separated, giving the impression she was praying and conveying the impression that even in death, Rosa Santos was more in touch with God than most people who were in attendance.

Rosa received her guests and after their visit, they could swear that she had spoken to them.

"Carlitos, mijito ama tu Angelita y Carlitos con todo tu corazón," Rosa greeted her son, the first visitor to hold court with his "Reina, the queen of his heart.

"Mama, te quiero con todo mi corazón, ya lo sabes. Rosa, la flor de mi corazón, yeah you already know that." Carlos leaned over the coffin and kissed her forehead. He struggled to keep from crying. She would not like him crying, however, a single tear rolled down to the tip of his nose and dropped on Rosa's hand.

Angélica walked up to Rosa's coffin and stared at her uncanny smiling face. Angélica felt a temperature change in her body; Rosa's smile sent coolness throughout her body. Angélica felt that Rosa had communicated with her; Rosa had touched her body and her spirit.

Juan Carlos rolled into the church and stopped beside the front row. He wanted to be positioned as close as possible to the coffin so that he could thank everyone for showing up to give Rosa her due respect.

The professional weepers started the crying, followed by the fifty-year old señoritas, so-called comadres, and the amigas that never spoke to Rosa and las mitoteras, the gossip queens, were 100 percent in attendance. They would not miss an opportunity to gather new material for their mitotes.

"Setenta cinco, nuestro padre que estas en el cielo...", continuously prayed the professional weepers at a dollar a prayer. In the chambers of the church, a seamless harmony of crying, praying aloud, and the choir singing melted softly into one another.

The boys' choir sang Avé María and it echoed off the ceiling. From a bird's eye view, the people's heads, the white roses in the women's hair and the men's lapels merged into the whiteness of a cumulus cloud.

As the migratory birds darken the sky, bringing with them signs of upcoming winds and rains, similarly, Mexican farm workers filled the highways bringing signs that the harvest season was about to start.

Berkeley, California, among the most famous and globally influential smallest community in the world, the city begins from the San Francisco bay and ascends gently up to the University of California campus and from there hurries up to the hills where the wealthy and the chancellor of the university live.

Boys grow up different than girls; boys develop friendships with other boys that are based on a common need to belong to a secret club: a secret society that creates its own history, develops it own code of ethics, and designs its own mythology with dragons to slay, battles to fight, and hideouts to disappear into.

Everyone is born to either live the life of a king, a queen, a beggar, a gardener, or a saint; Rosario, Doña Ro was slated to be a saint.

Ignacio had a wonderful smile and his copper hair made him look like an angel. The Bishop liked to surround himself with angels.

The Chinese populations in the Chinatowns were devastated by the massive deportations over the years, severing family lineages to such disrepair that they viewed themselves as loose railroad ties.

The full moon was in the early evening sky when the Oakland Raiders in their Silver and Black burst out of the locker room and out into the howling Raider Nation, that unruly alliance whose incomprehensible noise transmitted only static over the air waves: men from all walks of life painted their faces black or silver, dressed as pirates, and skeletons, all growled at the moon.

Carlos stepped up to the podium. He had prepared a lengthy eulogy for his mother. He had so much to say. He knew that he was not going to cry, Rosa had taught him not to cry or make noise regardless of how horrible things got. He had been prepared for this moment, watching his mother get brutalized by men, and yet remain silent.

"No Lloro porque te vas, ni lloro porque to alejas, lloro ahi si porque me dejas, herido del corazón." Ya se va la Embarcación finished playing and Carlos took the microphone: "I'm not crying because you left, nor am I crying because you went far away, I'm crying because you left me with a broken heart! I love those words! Thank you for coming today to honor the life of Rosa Santos, my mother. I, Carlos Santos, her only child, stand before you as a member of the Oakland Police Department. I credit my mother for my success. She always told me, 'Mijito, become alquien que la communidad respete! Become someone who the community will respect.' Because she loved dearly, she sacrificed everything, from her education to her reputation to give me a future."

190

"Well, today is a time to cry, a time to reflect, a time to forgive, and a time to give. Rosa Santos was a rose, a flower, Xochitl, the twentieth day of the Aztec calendar, a day for creating beauty and truth, especially that which speaks to the heart, because the heart knows it will one day cease to beat. And it was with this realization that Rosa lived life to the fullest."

The audience laughed through some of the eulogy and cried for most of it. Some in attendance trembled that Carlos might implicate them and cause a personal scandal; in the end, they were greatly relieved that the eulogy did not offend anyone; in fact they were thanked for loving Rosa Santos.

"Mom used to say," Carlos paused for a while and the whole place went mute, even the birds in the tile roof stopped cooing. His voice cracked on the first word but he recovered and was able to continue. "Trabajaba para que no le falte nada, mi hijo, I worked so that my son would not go without. First, she thought of the welfare of her son, Carlos and then her husband, Juan Carlos.

"I will always remember the aroma of her kitchen: the smell of refried beans, tamales, and fresh tortillas, and fresh brewed coffee. The foundation that she laid for me, I will always cherish, as well as her example, lighting a candle for an important event or to request a miracle from La Virgin de Guadalupe. When I took the exams in college, I called and asked her to light a candle for me. I know that her altar always had three candles glowing in the night, one for Carlitos, her grandson, one for me and one for her husband, Juan Carlos." Juan Carlos waived at everyone.

Rosalinda's daughter, Coca, a member of the United States Air force, dressed in an officer's uniform, stood up from her seat and scooted down the row, stepped into the aisle, and walked up to Rosa's coffin and saluted. She bent down and kissed her forehead. Rosa, "thank you, you were real!" She kissed her again, saluted and returned to the nearest available seat. Another greeting line was forming. Jimmy, son of Yiwu Yungfu Zhou and Rosalinda walked

191

up to Rosa.

"Hey, Rosa, you are the most beautiful flower in the rose garden, just ask Rosalinda and Yiwu!"

Rosalinda followed, holding on to her son, Jimmy and Yiwu, "Rosa, thank you for helping my family make ends meet. I know that you did not always sell the roses I brought for you to sell at your cantina." Yiwu smiled and cried; the strong man who never showed his feelings had one tear after another roll down his round face.

"Rosalinda, you can't imagine how happy I am for you and Yiwu. He really loves you, I can tell by the quality of the roses he groves for you. Yiwu will take good care of you and you will blossom too," reassured Rosa.

Rosario de Campos waited for everyone else in la familia to give Rosa their respect before her immediate family took their turn. Doña Ro prepared her cane to stand up and everyone nearby noticed. She and Don Robo stood up, the music stopped, the pigeons stopped cooing a second time and people stopped talking. Seven of her children and their families stood up, followed by Cristina, her sister. When Rosario, Doña Ro stepped out on to the aisle, Father Ignacio stood up and the rest of the people in the church also stood up.

Nobody was more grateful to Rosa Santos than Rosario, for curing her husband, Roberto of womanizing. The wild horse that Roberto had been in his youth was broken down to an old stallion that now circles the corral. While he was not able to show his love to anyone, he was at least at home, visible and able to do housework, repair the car, and guide the family without having to steer it. That had become Rosario's role. He looked down at Rosa's smiling face and smiled back. "I promise to honor Rosario for the rest of my life. Thank you for showing me the way, I was lost until I met you, Rosa." Don Robo felt that Rosa was smiling at him. Without saying another word, he stepped aside to let Rosario get closer to Rosa and he continued to look down at Rosa.

Rosario touched Rosa's wrinkled hand, held it, and kissed her forehead. "Go in peace my friend. Vaya con Dios!" Rosario prayed, "*The Lord is my shepherd, I lack nothing. He makes me lie down in green pastures, he leads me beside quite waters, and he refreshes my soul. He guides me along the rights paths for his name's sake. Even though I walk through the darkest valley, I will fear no evil, for you are with me; your rod and your staff, they comfort me. You prepare a table before me in the presence of my enemies. You anoint my head with oil; my cup overflows. Surely your goodness and love will follow me all the days of my life, and I will dwell in the house of the Lord.*"

She wanted to stay longer and visit with Rosa, but with the pressure of the long line of people waiting to see Rosa, she took Don Robo's arm and walk a ways to sit with Rosa's family.

*   *   *   *   *

Toward the end of 2012, the media and most of western civilization were extraordinarily focused on the correlation between the end of the 13th B'ak'tun on the Mayan calendar and December 21-23, 2012 on the Gregorian calendar. Some self-anointed experts warned of the coming of a cataclysmic event, supposedly predicted by the ancient Mayans. When nothing happened, the media once again displayed their short attention span and reverted to the next most compelling topic, the Serial Killer's Killer, still very much at large.

"Will SKK execute another criminal? When and where?" The media did not trust law enforcement to reveal important future details of SKK's executions. A rumor was circulating that law enforcement had captured SKK, and secretly disposed of him, because SKK was a law enforcement officer, and they could not afford any more collateral damage.

The briefing room in the San Francisco Police Department was buzzing with allegations that heads were rolling. The media in the Bay Area continued to broadcast allegations of incompetence of those in charge of the police departments and throughout the Bay Area. It was shocking that after so many years, law enforcement still had no idea who the Serial Killers' Killer might be. Speculations that the legal system protected criminals in and out of jail, enhanced the public popularity of the Serial Killers' Killer. The media was relentless: every television station in the bay area ran segments on SKK. The media created a folk hero out of SKK for having successfully executed serial killers in their society and the fallout hit the Berkeley Police Department. Captain Williams was removed from his assignment and replaced by a FBI agent, who was given total authority. The FBI also governed over the San Francisco Police Department.

CNN: In California, a serial killer has gained the popularity of a folk hero, the Serial Killers' Killer has taken 12 lives over the course of thirty years and law enforcement has no clue of whom might be committing these murders. SKK is known to construct altars for each of his homicides and decorate them with offerings: roses, funeral urns, candles, and art pieces. At each homicide, SKK has left clues, giving police the location of the next kill and still they fail to capture him. SKK is so elusive that he may be hiding among the police departments, someone working for the police in some capacity. An insider would explain how he knows so much about each person he executes. The last homicide credited to SKK did not reveal any evidence of where SKK may strike next. Either the police is keeping information from the media or SKK has elected to stop the killing.

Chinese New Years, the year of the Snake, was approaching and law enforcement focused on the parade. Undercover federal security flooded the streets weeks before the parade. If SKK copycats had any plans, they were most certainly discouraged by the amount of security.

Two blocks away from where the parade, a black van drove through an alley and parked next to a stairway that led to apartments on the second and third floors. From the streets, a man dressed in black was seen unloading furniture and black plastic bags and climbing the stairs with the bags. The van drove away, but an hour later, the man reappeared climbing the stairs. The rooftop apartment had a patio with an arbor decorated with plants and Chinese antique furniture. The mysterious stranger nailed a white canvas to one side of the arbor and placed a life size terracotta soldier to protect it. A funerary art piece made from wooden Chinese characters was centered on the altar and candles illuminated the base. A colorful life-size La Virgen de Guadalupe was facing East with her back to the Bay Bridge.

From the patio, Oakland and Berkeley lit the sky with different colored lights. The cables from the Bay Bridge reflected a bright grey from the full moon. The man dressed in black placed four two-foot candles between smaller terracotta soldiers and smaller candles placed with precision throughout the garden. He painted the front door and the window frames red. A two-foot framed votive art piece was tacked to a post on the patio. At that point, the beginning of the Chinese New Year's procession stole the attention of neighbors idly observing the unfolding of the strange tableau. The night was beginning to set in and people throughout Chinatown were in their places ready to watch the parade.

While others were occupied, darkness in the arbor ceremonially vanquished, one small candle at a time, followed with chants and silent prayer. More candles were placed in line with the front of the altar. The man moved slowly in front of the altar, the music played softly in the background as he continued to light the two-foot candles. After lighting all the candles, the man faced the soldiers and performed Tai Chi while Chinese flutes and strings played in the background. He stopped, bowed, and stepped forward to light the funerary art piece. The wicks in the candelabra lit easily. He bowed again and stood motionless until the music stopped.

With his back to the universe and facing the statues he took off his black body shirt, a hood, slipped his black gloves off his hands and dropped them at the foot of the altar where Dzidzat was being observed. The fireworks exploded as the Chinese New Year's parade started and the burning of paper filled the area with smoke. Except for his black socks, the kind that surgeons wear, he was completely naked and painted black from head to toe. The cracking and snapping noises grew louder as he doubled over in pain. His black painted body began to peel.

The funerary art piece burst into flames and ignited the wooden fence adjacent to the arbor. The flames jumped from board to board along the fence until it jumped onto the next-door neighbor's house. The doubled-over man screamed as the skin peeled off his body and the fire raced up to the roof of the neighbor's house. Because of the fireworks during the Chinese New Year's parade, the fire department was already on high alert, and within fifteen minutes, the firemen were spraying water on the burning building.

The fire chief traced the origin of the fire to the arbor in a neighbor's backyard. Having attended a briefing on SKK, the chief directed his officers to investigate the neighbor's house for the probability of a connection. After speaking with the neighbors, they discovered that the owners of the house were away visiting relatives in China and that the house was unoccupied at the time of the fire.

A police officer, first on the scene, identified some of SKK's signature items left in the arbor: thirteen white roses were carefully arranged in a half circle in front of the terracotta soldiers and a funerary art piece from Bo Nianzu's collection. Most definitely, all evidence was part of SKK's signature.

Diego was the lead detective on the investigation of homicides committed by SKK, other detectives in the Bay Area communicated with him on a regular basis on any leads which could conceivably shed light on the SKK case.

At 3:00am, Diego received a call from SFPD, "Detective de Campos?" asked a SFPD detective.

"Yes, this is Detective de Campos," answered Diego with slurred speech.

"We identified a possible homicide in China Town with a possible connection to SKK."

"What is the location of the crime scene?" asked Diego as he rushed out the door, grabbing a mug of reheated coffee from Chi as the door closed behind him.

The alley was jammed with police cars flashing red and blue lights in the white foggy night, all with their spotlights aimed at the arbor. Diego got out of the car and walked in a calm fashion to the backyard entrance to the crime scene. The white canvas flapped in the cool breeze that whispered in the night. About eight people worked around the crime scene. He walked around the perimeter of the arbor and stopped behind the canvas to observe the car spotlights shining through the canvas exposing a larger than life image of Jesús Christ standing with his right arm bent at the elbow. The front of the arbor was decorated with statues of saints and the terracotta soldiers of different sizes, and an accompanying funerary art structure that was badly burned. SKK was most definitely connected to this crime scene. On the front of the altar, thirteen white roses were arranged in a six by six foot area. A pile of black clothes rested inside the arch of the patio.

As Diego knelt, he smelled the strong odor of lavender and burnt wax. With the handle of his flashlight, he separated the black clothes: a pair of leggings, a hood, gloves, and a long-sleeved shirt. With latex gloves, he picked up the shirt with the club and observed it while turning it. He slowly and methodically turned it inside out, and fish-like scales fell out of it.

The shirt was placed on a table that set up by the forensics team. A large piece of snakeskin was pulled out of the shirt. The first thought Diego had on the Year of the Snake, the Dragon had shed his own skin, Evil had transformed. Diego vowed to follow Evil into the afterlife if it meant that he could defeat it. He shivered as he said to himself, "Fear not Evil."

A forensics technician alerted Diego that he had found something sewed into the fabric of the body shirt. The technician cut through the fabric and with tweezers pulled out a high school picture of a young attractive Mexican girl. The picture had been worn on the left pectoral, next to the suspect's heart. The back of the picture read, "Para mi Caballo Blanco, Te Amo, Rosa Rita Galindo and it was dated June 16, 1966. At last, we might be finding a semblance of a motive, thought Diego. *Perhaps SKK and Rosa Rita Galindo were once sweethearts and something, or someone prevented them from loving each* other.

The morning light was helping forensics do a better job of collecting evidence. The statues were removed and the canvas with the drawing of Jesús was taken down and packed in a truck. Nianzu's funerary art was carefully packed inside a black van and driven away. The votive painting was still tacked to the arbor's post. A closer look at the painting, showed a police officer choking a large snake. Diego took a last look at the painting and noticed that the snake was shedding its skin and white scales were falling off the snake. A warm sensation dispersed throughout Diego's body with the realization that the puzzle pieces of the Rose cases were coming together and filling in the details of the story behind the Serial Killer's Killer. Diego concluded since the crime scene did not have a body it ruled out a homicide, and recorded the crime scene as arson. The crime scene was scattered with SKK's signature, including his clothes. Diego thought that perhaps, whoever SKK is, he is trying to tell us that SKK symbolically killed himself and that he no longer exists.

Diego called Chi and left a voice mail that he was driving to Gilroy to talk to his friend James Peace.

James and Diego met at the donut shop by the middle school on First Street, James's favorite place in the whole world. Jame's shift as security guard began in two hours, which gave them plenty of time to talk.

"James, do you know anything about the Galindo family from the mid-sixties?" asked Diego not wasting any time.

"Good to see you Diego! How's the family?" asked James, showing Diego that courtesy was still expected in their friendship.

"Fine, but do you remember the Galindo's family from the sixties?" asked Diego exhibiting some frustration and impatience.

"Lemmee see, from what I can recall, the Galindos were one of the families escorted out of the county by the garlic farmer's association. Yes! I think, I remember something about INS trying to deport them, but four of the children were born in Hollister, and therefore, were American citizens."

"Was one of the girls named Rosa Rita?" asked Diego.

"Yes, as a matter of fact, there was a Rosa... Rita, but she went by Rita. Rosa Rita was quite a good-looking young lady," James noted."

"Why would they want to relocate the family?" asked Diego.

James continues, "Well, you just hit it, Rosa Rita was a pretty

198

girl. I believe that a grandson of a wealthy farmer, who fell in love with her. The families could not keep the lovers apart so they separated them."

James took a big bite of his donut and a mouthful of coffee to wash it down. "Yeah, I think I remember. I say that because I am no longer Mr. Archives. I think I remember the Galindos, and I'm pretty sure the Gilroy Garlic Association relocated them to another state, yes, Texas, Texas."

Diego returned home, shared his thoughts of SKK with Chi, ate breakfast, showered and rushed to the office to share his findings with the Berkeley Police Department's SKK team. For months on end, they had briefings on SKK, but despite their best efforts, they could find no further clues related to the identity of SKK nor could they locate the Galindo family in Texas or any other state in the country. Perhaps the family went back to México or the relocation also included changing the Galindos identity by giving them a different surname.

The search for the Serial Killer's Killer turned into a thick dark cloud that rolled over the city and the Golden Gate Bridge and just sat there waiting for the earth to turn so that it could reveal once again the physical and emotional attraction that people have towards San Francisco and the Golden Gate Bridge.

The morning light quickly ate away the darkness. The sun was striking the molecules in the atmosphere and scattering the blue hue in greater quantities than the other colors; turning the sky a little bit bluer with each passing minute.

Epilogue

Five Years Later:

A security guard rings the doorbell to my house in the Oakland Hills overlooking the Golden Gate Bridge. It is a warm summer morning. Before it gets too hot to work outside, I am on the back patio with a laptop computer editing journal entries of my twenty years as a detective for the Berkeley Police Department. From the patio, in full splendor, the bright orange bridge spans the horizon.

"Good morning Detective Ling!" greets an officer from the Berkeley Police Department. "Officer Johnson, BPD," he introduces himself, and hands Chi a package for "Detective de Campos," the officer tips his hat, and walks back to the gate where he had parked his car.

Chi places the package on a coffee table next to me, it is a small black cardboard box with a green ribbon tied into a bow. I look over the top of the computer and focus on the box. The FBI sticker on it indicated that they had inspected the package. I pick up the box and immediately notice that it was so lightweight and it appears to be empty. I untie the ribbon and open the box. Inside was a used Wilson tennis ball. I stand up, take the yellow ball out of the box, walk away from the table and bounce the ball against the patio floor.

The sound of the tennis ball bouncing filled my mind with the memory of standing at the back entrance of the Claremont Hotel, and listening to the tennis players' grunts as they hit the ball back and forth to each other.

"Ugh!"

"Agh!"

"Ugh!"

Father Ignacio's prayer at Rosa's funeral resonated," *The Lord is my shepherd, I lack nothing. He makes me lie down in green pastures, he leads me beside quite waters, and he refreshes my soul. …..*

I squeeze the tennis ball and pray, "In the presence of our enemies, we will Fear Not Evil, for the Lord will protect those of us who are pure at heart. In the name of the Hoppers, I promise that I will not rest until I capture you," with resolve I tighten the grip on the tennis ball and continue bouncing it.

About the Storyteller

Arturo Muñoz Vásquez was born in Piedras Negras, Coahuila, Mexico. During his childhood, his family immigrated to the United States as seasonal farm workers. The family settled in Gilroy, California where they were able to find year around work in the fruit orchards and garlic fields. The migrant life style provided Arturo with much of the material for his storytelling and storybooks. Storytelling came natural to him early in life, while still dressed in only underwear children gathered around to listen attentively to his wild and silly stories. As a limited English speaker in the Texas public school, he was disciplined for speaking Spanish, which resulted in diminishing his enthusiasm to become a storyteller. Although he struggled to become English proficient, he excelled in sports, becoming the captain of the wrestling team and defensive captain of the football team. Through high school and college, teachers and professors returned his essays and term papers bleeding with red ink. One professor told him that his term paper was the worst written essay he had ever graded. Serendipity, a turn of events took place, professor Jimenez from the Chicano Studies Program at San Jose State, handed Arturo his **A** term paper on the **Teachings of Quetzalcoatl**, it also had red marks on it and terms papers from other students with no red marks on them, received lower grades. When challenged the professor commented, " He had something to say!" This acknowledgement of his storytelling abilities fueled his inspiration to become a storyteller.

About the Author

His unpublished writings include: a novel written over forty years ago *Playa Negra*, a love story about a black sand beach engulfed with white sand beaches, the crystalline waters, coral riffs, exotic animals (such as the Quetzal bird), volcanoes and wild jungles which seduce travelers with an aphrodisiac found in Costa Rica known as "La Pura Vida". He wrote short stories for storytelling performances: some of these include *Where Are My Children, A Retold Story of La Llorona, Faster than a Speeding Chicken, A Christmas Tragedy, Matli as Punk Kid, and A Tour of Insults.* His first published children's book, **Papá, Tell us Another Story, a Collection of Bedtime Stories** that were written from the storytelling time he spent nightly with his sons, Simeon and Nataniel. As district superintendent in Hoopa, California he wrote, **Add More Water to the Beans** and **Running Deer Plays Hooky**, a story about a Native American boy who found learning to read difficult; he also noticed the shortage of high interest books for middle school age students, inspired him to write, *A* **Storyteller's Nightmare.**

It is with a great deal of excitement that he unveils this murder mystery, **FEAR NOT EVIL**, *and provides you with a glimpse of its sequel,* **Where Light is Darker Than Night**. *In the sequel, detective Diego de Campos must travel into the afterlife to chase and capture the Serial Killer's Killer.*